OUTCAST

SEAL Team: Disavowed - Book Two

LAURA MARIE
ALTOM

Outcast
Copyright © January 2016 by Laura Marie Altom

SEAL Team: Disavowed series

To become a United States Navy SEAL, a man must be physically forged in steel and able to mentally compute life or death situations with laser accuracy and speed. Our country trusts these men with the most sensitive military operations—many so covert that once they are successfully completed, they are never spoken of again.

This series celebrates one particularly fierce band of brothers who valiantly battled terrorists whose crimes against nature and humanity were far too great to chance escape. On a dark night, on foreign soil, SEAL Team Alpha witnessed acts so unspeakably cruel against women, infants and small children that their consciences would not allow anything other than their own brand of justice for the scum terrorist cell.

A trial would have been too good for these pigs, and so, one-by-one they were taken out, and the women and children they'd used were freed. By dawn, an entire region breathed easier. The men of Alpha found themselves heroes to those whose lives they had saved, but virtual criminals in the eyes of the organization they served. After a lengthy investigation, their elite, covert team was formally disbanded.

They now spend their lives deep undercover, still serving—no longer their country, but individuals who find themselves in need of not only their own personal warrior, but a particular brand of justice.

While honorably discharged, these men and their actions will forever be *disavowed* . . .

SEAL Team: Disavowed series

1

"They're all dead . . ." English lit professor, Eden Marabella, dropped the satellite phone she'd been speaking into. It shattered against the rocks at her feet, but shock at the sight before her made the loss of their team's primary outside communication tool a non-issue.

Her throat closed with emotion. Her eyes stung.

The more of the grisly scene she digested, the more her stomach roiled.

She retched at the sheer amount of blood spilled across the ice. It had frozen in pools beneath the majestic creatures, standing in stark contrast to the Orcas' beautiful black and white markings.

Her father's work partner and long-time family friend, Dane Northrup, a marine biologist from

Stony Brook University in New York, slipped his arm around her shoulders, comforting her through her latest round of nausea. "Deep breaths," he coached. "Ride it out."

"W-what happened?" she asked, her voice shallow and dazed. "It looks like an entire pod." Dozens of killer whales had washed up upon the snow and ice-crusted shore of their stretch of Antarctica's Ross Sea. Her father, a marine biology professor from the University of Tampa had been coming here for years. He and his students had raised millions for conservation and research and now had a private station manned year-round with students and scientists pursuing independent studies.

Her poor father silently moved among the beached creatures as if under a dark spell. His shoulders slumped. Silent tears glistened on his ruddy cheeks in the bright November sun.

The day was a rare jewel with the temperature almost above freezing and the horizon clear. Tragedy didn't happen on perfect afternoons like this, so why were they facing so much death now?

Earlier that morning, Eden and her dad had caught a ride from friends stationed at McMurdo. Dane followed with her father's other business partner, Leo Adler, and two students who'd opted to stay in their rooms to get settled.

The walk to the beach had become an annual tradition for Eden, Dane, and her father. One typically highlighted by visiting an Adélie penguin colony on the rocky point. In her shock over the orcas, she'd forgotten them. She was now afraid to glance in that direction.

"Dane," she turned to him, selfishly wishing he were Jasper, the sweetheart she'd been dating back in Denver. She'd been on the sat phone leaving a heartfelt message for him, trying to explain why she'd broken things off, when she'd crested the last rise on the shore trail to witness the carnage below. "Could you please check the penguins? I can't . . ."

"Eden, I'm sorry, but—"

"How did this happen?" Her sob cut off his words. The instant she'd heard his apology, she'd made the mistake of looking for herself.

The penguins were dead, too.

Dane grasped her upper arms to keep her from collapsing onto her knees. "I promise we'll get to the bottom of this. I won't rest till we have an answer."

She nodded.

When he wrapped his arms around her for a hug, it only reminded her how much she missed Jasper. Until now, she hadn't realized how great a role he'd played in her life—not that it mattered.

She'd never see him again.

She wasn't even sure why she'd called, other than that she loved this place more than any other in the world. On what would no doubt be her last visit, she'd wanted to share it with him.

That said, at the moment the man who needed her most was her grief-stricken father who wept over the lifeless penguin chick he cradled in his palms.

Eden had only taken two steps in his direction when the ground began to shake.

2

Four days later . . .

W̶hat had he been thinking?

Disavowed Navy SEAL Jasper King jumped down from the snowcat he'd spent the past four hours riding on from McMurdo Station, then raised his gloved hand to his forehead, shielding his eyes from the glare of sun on snow. For as far as he could see—which, granted, wasn't all that far with frigid wind swirling patches of white stuff into an otherworldly haze—was a whole lot of nothing. If not for the fact that he was currently jacked up on bad coffee and concern for his friend, the vast sea of white stretching in front of him would have sent him packing for that little slice of Bahamian heaven he was all the time dreaming about.

The thing was, the more he'd been around Eden, the more he realized he was no longer content with his usual daydream of chilling on the beach with a longneck *Kalik*. He wanted to do that chilling with the only woman who'd made him think twice about his vow to remain single—like his brother.

Sure, what happened to his brother's wife, Mariah, had been an accident, but that hadn't kept Jasper from becoming a pariah to his family. An outcast. Clearly, he couldn't bring her back so his plan was to spend a lonely lifetime punishing himself in the same way he'd unwittingly punished Kyle—his older brother by five years.

Jasper wasn't proud of the mistakes he'd made back then.

He'd been a rebellious punk, making one reckless, stupid decision after another until reaching the point that he could no longer trust his inner voice. If you couldn't trust yourself, you had no one. Which was pretty much the emotional place where Jasper had been when joining the Navy.

Ten years later, his decision-making skills had been honed, yet every so often, doubts still crept in. Like the one dogging him about why he was even here.

He tried forcing a deep breath of the air that hovered in negative double digits, but it burned his lungs, so he jerked up the zipper on his government-issued red parka, slipped on mirrored Ray-Bans, and then followed his driver, Doug, toward the modular prefab research station where Eden and her dad supposedly worked.

"How long's it been since you heard from them?" Jasper asked on the approach to the station's outer door.

"Three days. I chatted with her father via email. Though comms are crashed down here more than they're up, so it's not all that unheard of. I'm sure they're fine, and you wasted a damned long trip just to check on your girl."

"She's not mine," Jasper bristled. He'd be lying if he said he didn't want her to be, but this was strictly a cautionary mission. Even if he had been inclined to see whatever he and Eden shared through to a mutually satisfying conclusion, she'd ended things between them before he'd had the chance.

"Whatever." Doug opened the door.

The sudden warmth screwed with Jasper's sinuses.

Doug removed his coat and snow pants, hanging both on a long rack that held at least a dozen more.

Jasper followed suit. He was antsy to see for himself that Eden was okay, but played it cool. Doug already thought he was an idiot. Jasper didn't want to look like one, too, by charging into the station like some half-cocked gedunk.

"Leave your boots, too." Doug pointed to Jasper's heavy black Sorels. "Quickest way to piss off a whole station is to track in snow."

"Thanks. Good to know."

Once both men stood in jeans, long-sleeved T-shirts and thick, white socks, Doug opened the station's inner door.

Jasper caught himself holding his breath.

He wasn't sure what to expect.

The only thing he knew for sure was that in this moment, his heart damn near beat out of his chest with anticipation. Screw his Joe Cool act. He couldn't wait to hold Eden in his arms. After that, he'd assess their relationship status.

He dropped the satchel holding his personal belongings to the vinyl floor.

"Strange . . ." Doug stepped deeper into the rectangular, white-walled space that looked like a rec room. Four long tables sat at one end while a pool table, sofa, big screen TV, and four pinball machines occupied the remaining space. A white plate holding a half-eaten sandwich and chips sat on an end table. Coffee cups, two jigsaw puzzles, and a few beer cans littered the other tabletops. "Usually, this place is hopping."

Jurassic Park played on the TV with the volume muted.

A splatter of red stood out on the nearest white,

prefab wall. Blood?

Warning bells clanged in Jasper's head. Maybe his trip down here hadn't been so foolish, after all.

"Guess they must have pulled an all-nighter. Everyone's crashed."

"Meaning we should do a bunk check." Jasper gravitated toward the splattered wall for a closer inspection, but then opted to save that for later. A more pressing issue was finding Eden—*now*.

"Yeah." Doug scratched his head. "Sure, I guess."

"Lead the way. I'm seeing two options." The station had been built with modular pods connected by short, dark spindly corridors that looked more like creepy tunnels.

"Let's take the one on the right. It leads to the labs. If the crew's not there, we'll check their rooms."

"Sounds like a plan. How many crew members are here?"

"Last count was thirty-seven. Most share rooms."

"Is that counting Eden and her dad?"

"Uh huh." They'd reached the hall and Doug flipped a switch that immersed the space in cool, florescent light. "Usually, these overheads are left on twenty-four seven."

Jasper didn't like where this was going. Why were thirty-seven people suddenly silent? The question made him rub the back of his neck.

A communal office area was empty, as were the first two labs. Each area sported signs of occupants—half-empty coffee mugs, an unfinished poker game and a worn paperback copy of *How to Win Friends and Influence People*.

"I don't know what to make of this . . ." Doug shook his head. "At first, I thought your concerns were screwy, but now I'm not so sure."

Jasper had opened his mouth to reply when a barrel-chested man emerged from one of the as yet unexplored labs at the end of the pod. His bulbous nose was red as if he'd blown it one too many times. Despite a large smile, his high forehead made his blue eyes appear mean.

Startled, the man lurched back, then laughed. "Doug, you scared the shit out of me. Why didn't you call?"

"Been trying for days. How's it going?" The two men shook hands.

"Couldn't be better. Up until this morning, the weather has been strangely cooperative, so most of the crew are camped at the beach."

"That explains it." Doug nodded. "Why this place is a ghost town."

"That's the reason. Sorry, I don't have a more exciting answer for you. I'm expecting them back any time." The giant man winked. His pale blue eyes looked almost white. Laugh lines at the corners led

Jasper to place him in the forty to fifty age range. Short, spiky blond hair stood at attention. Jeans and a khaki, long-sleeved Columbia PFG made him look more like an explorer than science-type. He extended his right hand for Jasper to shake. "I'm Leo— resident marine biologist guru extraordinaire. And you are . . ."

Jasper introduced himself, then explained, "I'm a friend of Eden Marabella. She around?"

"As a matter of fact, she is. But she worked so long last night on her great American novel that about thirty minutes ago she hit her bunk for a nap."

"A nap?" The Eden he knew was a powerhouse. Always full of energy and ready for her next adventure. "Point me toward her room. She won't mind me waking her."

"Afraid I can't do that," Leo said with a clucking sound and slight shake of his head. "You see, she really has overdone it lately. As her supervisor, for her own well-being, I think it would be best if you—"

"Know what I think best?" Jasper asked with a less-than-cordial tone. "If you'd show me the way to her room."

"Of course." Unfazed by Jasper's attitude, he turned back toward the lab. "Give me a moment to wrap up my latest project. It's time sensitive."

"Whatever." Jasper waved him along. "Hurry." He hadn't meant to come across like an ass with Eden's coworker, but the guy rubbed him the wrong way. Something was hinky down here, and before he left, he'd figure out what. In the meantime, he'd feel a whole lot better once he saw for himself that Eden was all right.

"Thank you for your patience," Leo said with an uber-polite formality that made Jasper's teeth hurt. The guy was up to no good. Jasper's gut typically never steered him wrong. "A few more seconds and . . ." A timer dinged. "There we go. All done. As soon as I jot down the results, we'll go."

A glance beyond a triple-paned window showed the landscape had vanished.

All that remained of the outside world was white.

Though it was plenty warm inside the station, Jasper shivered. The sooner he got out of here, the better. The whole place gave him the creeps. Even more than he hated being duped, he hated being cold. Experiencing both in the same day had him twitchy—never a good thing when he'd been forbidden to carry firepower on what was supposed to be a scientific expedition.

"It's looking pretty bad." Doug folded his arms. "Should you radio the crew? What if they're lost in that whiteout?"

"No worries." Leo rose from his workstation stool. "I'm sure they're safe and sound."

"How can you say that? It's a mess out there."

"Trust me . . ." Leo's smile held all the warmth

of the nearest iceberg. "They won't feel a thing. And neither will you once you join them." He pulled a 9mm out from behind test tubes and a Bunsen burner.

"Hey, whoa . . ." Doug raised his hands and backed away. "What the hell? There are no guns allowed down here. And we've been friends for like what? Six years?"

Leo shrugged. "We'll part as friends."

Was this actually going down?

"Both of you," Leo waved the gun to herd them toward the door. "Into the hall. I don't want blood in my workspace."

With his Glock stuck back in New Zealand, Jasper opted for the next best thing. The moment Leo averted his gaze, Jasper grabbed a test tube, flinging the contents in the guy's ugly face. He'd hoped to get lucky with a shot of acid, but the benign liquid merely pissed Leo off.

"That wasn't wise." Their host used the back of his shirtsleeve to wipe down his face.

"Where's Eden?" Leo's inattention became Jasper's advantage. He leapt toward him, wrenching the gun from his hand.

Leo lurched forward to take back the weapon, but Jasper used the man's momentum to swing him around. With one arm securing Leo in a backwards chokehold, Jasper used his free hand to grind the gun's business-end against his temple. Whispering into his ear, he asked, "*Where is she?*"

"You're outnumbered," Leo said. "My associates will be here momentarily to dispense with you."

Jasper tightened his hold. "Where. Is. Eden?"

Leo had the nerve to laugh, so Jasper choked the air from his throat long enough to cause him to pass out.

Pinning him to the floor, Jasper asked Doug, "Find me something to tie him up with."

For a precious few seconds, Doug appeared dumbfounded, but then surged into action. Furiously opening drawers, only to slam them closed. He finally held up a roll of duct tape. "Will this work?"

"Yep. Thanks." Jasper rolled the tape around Leo's wrists and ankles.

Finished, he tucked the 9mm in the waistband of his jeans.

"Who are you?" Doug asked with a tremble to his voice.

With a half laugh, Jasper dragged the unconscious Leo to a storage closet. "I could be your best friend or your worst enemy. Choose."

"Look, man," he backed toward the door. "I'm in way over my head. Let's grab Eden and hop in my ride. Once we're back at McMurdo, we'll report this to the authorities and figure out what to do from there."

"Sorry, pal. At the moment, I'm the closest thing to an authority you've got." Jasper surveyed the mess even the brief struggle had made. "Unless you have an arsenal stashed on your ride, once this guy's friends show up, we might be in a world of hurt." He jogged for the hall, brushed past Doug, then shouted, *"Eden!* Babe, where are you?"

Doug chased after him. "Have you considered the possibility that he killed her?"

"No." Through room after room, Jasper searched. *"Eden!"*

"You should have asked why Leo had a gun."

"Eden! Answer me!" In the two-story dormitory pod, Jasper kicked in door after door. If something had happened to her. . .

He didn't like thinking of the violence he was capable of doing, but if he discovered that bastard had hurt Eden, he'd annihilate him.

"Think about it," Doug persisted. "Why would a world-renowned scientist who's been studying in Antarctica practically longer than I've been alive be waving a gun around? And what did he mean about all those team members not *feeling* anything? You don't think he killed them, do you? I mean, you hear about people going off the deep end down here, but that usually just means too much booze or sleeping around. I've never encountered anything like this."

"Eden!" His companion talked too damned much.

Jasper tried the next door on the right and found it locked, so he kicked it in, only to freeze.

Eden lay stretched across a twin bed with her neck crooked at an unnatural angle. Her wrists and ankles had been bound with zip ties. He felt like he was going to puke.

Am I already too late?

3

"Talk to me, babe . . ."

Eden was vaguely aware of Jasper's take-charge tone, but it drifted to her on a foggy dream.

"You still have that sat phone in your cat?"

"Yeah . . ."

"Then don't just stand there—get outside and call McMurdo. She needs medical help, and God only knows what that sicko did with the rest of the crew."

"Right. Sure."

Who belonged to the second, unsure voice? She couldn't place him.

"Eden, talk to me. Did Leo do this to you?"

Tugs at her feet and wrists told her the restraints that had forced her muscles to seize had finally been removed. She groaned in relief, only to wince when her limbs painfully tingled at the sudden movement.

Her eyelids fluttered open, and she licked her dry lips. She took in her surroundings and then it all rushed back—screams. Chaos. Painful silence and uncertainty as she struggled to decide if she were dead or alive. "Jasper? W-what are you doing here?"

"Isn't that obvious?" He perched on the edge of the bed, cupping his hand to her cheek. "I'm here to rescue you, and from looks of it, not a moment too soon. What the hell happened? When your message ended so abruptly, I figured something had gone wrong, but this . . ." He whistled.

He offered her a freshly opened bottled water. She drank it all.

"Leo—he lost it." Her breakup with Jasper had been hard enough, but what had happened since didn't seem possible. Like she'd wake to realize it had all been a nightmare. "He's been one of my father's closest friends and coworkers forever. The day I called you, I'd wanted to explain why I broke things off, but then . . ." Crushing memories returned. "W-we found an entire pod of dead Orcas washed ashore. Penguins, too. My father was inconsolable. He wouldn't eat or sleep for two days. Then he and Leo and Dane—his other partner—locked themselves in Leo's lab, and there was arguing, but none of us could make out much of what they were saying."

"You said, 'us', as in you weren't alone. How

many people were you with, and where are they now? Leo mentioned something about them doing research on a nearby beach. Do they need help?"

She shook her head, and then squeezed her stinging eyes closed. Blood. So much blood. As long as she lived, she'd never erase their screams from her heart.

"Once my dad and Dane left the lab, the energy between them was tense. It was lunchtime, and everyone but them either stood in line for their meal or had already sat down to eat. I-I'm not sure where my dad and Dane went from there, but at the start of *The Price is Right*'s showcase—we watch a recorded feed every day to make us feel closer to home—six men came into the station. Hulking men. They were dressed all in white, and didn't take off their winter gear—not even their boots. I remember thinking, *Why are they wearing white? They're just asking for trouble if they're ever lost in a storm.*" She took a deep breath. "At first when the men showed up, there was a general hum of excited chatter. We don't get much company down here, you know? A few of our guys strolled over to greet them." She wiped silent tears with the backs of her hands. "Leo strode in from his lab—whistling. He made eye contact with one of the new guys, and then nodded. And then . . ." Her inhalations quickened to the point that she had trouble catching her breath.

"Take a break," Jasper urged. "You don't have to

tell me everything now."

"I do," she said with a firm nod. "I have to get it out of me. After Leo gave his men that nod, he scurried like the rat he is back to his lab. But the rest of us . . ." She shuddered. "We sat there like proverbial fish in a barrel while each one of those men withdrew handguns and started firing. It took a few seconds for those of us still alive to react. I mean, we were stunned. Then there was too much noise— screaming and shouting. The clang of chairs being knocked over. Firecracker pops from the guns. My friends who tried running were shot in their backs. I ducked under a table, holding my arms over my head." Trapped in the memory, she adopted the same pose now. "Then it got quiet. The only sound over my pulse was the gameshow's theme song playing during the closing credits." She pressed her hand to her chest. "My heart beat so hard and fast I believed I'd die from fright. I'd never been so scared. I squeezed my eyes shut, pretending everything was going to be okay. Then I heard footsteps. I opened my eyes to find a pair of white boots stepping toward me—only they were splattered with blood. One of the shooters crouched, gesturing for me to come out. I shook my head. He said something in a language I didn't understand. Maybe German? I tried scooting away, but another man shoved chairs away from the table, then grabbed me from behind. With his hands under my arms, he dragged me to the nearest chair. I fought him—kicking and clawing. But then another guy pointed a gun in my face and I stilled."

Jasper stroked her hair. "I'm sorry I wasn't here for you. For all of you."

She sniffed and nodded, leaning against his warm, solid chest. "For what seemed like forever, I sat in that chair. Stone still. All around me, there was motion. Four men hauled my friends outside as if they were trash. More men had removed their winter gear to scrub blood from the chairs and tables and floor. More men clanged about in the kitchen— cooking a meal. I felt frozen. Locked in time and space. I once tried escaping, hoping to find my dad and Dane, but before I left the chair, the guy with the gun ground the barrel against my ear. Leo returned. By that time, the rec room once again looked normal. Leo pulled up a chair across from me—as if he expected a cozy chat." She laughed and shook her head. "He fired off question after question about what my father was hiding. None of it made sense. I kept telling him I didn't know, but then he started raving about it being his *turn* and how it was time to *rewrite history*. He insisted I tell him where my dad stashed *it*, and when I told him I didn't have a clue what he was talking about, he screamed at me about my father's secret *source*."

"And by *source*, you have no idea what he meant?"

She shook her head. "If all I'd had to do to save dozens of lives was tell him, don't you think I would have from the start? He's crazy. The men he works with are worse. Heartless."

Expression grim, he pulled her into his arms. She clung to him. What kind of man flew to Antarctica merely because he had a suspicion that a woman might be in trouble? Jasper was kind and considerate. Fearless. The first time he'd touched his lips to hers, she'd had the oddest sensation of having found home. But then she'd gotten her diagnosis and—she couldn't bear thinking of what was to come.

Why hadn't Leo and his men shot her and gotten it over with?

That's why she'd ended things with Jasper. The disease's inevitability.

Even as a little girl, she'd been the practical one. When her mother had been sick and her father was desperately searching for a miracle cure, Eden had no choice but to grow up fast.

"We'll figure this out, okay?"

She nodded.

"Where are your father and Dane now?"

"I don't know. I haven't seen either of them since the killing started. That was one—maybe two—days ago. I think at some point Leo drugged me. It's all messed up in my mind."

"Speaking of the bastard," Jasper pulled away. "I should check on him and Doug. Want to tag along or stay here?"

"I'll stay with you." The idea of being away from him, if only briefly, left her feeling bereft. *Way to stick to your convictions.* How many times had she told herself that staying away from him was the kindest thing she could do? Yet, she never could have seen this coming.

"Sure you're feeling up to walking around?"

"I think so. Regardless, I don't want to be left alone."

"Fair enough." He stood, then held out his hands to help her from the bed. "Take it slow."

She was dizzy at first, but a few deep breaths cleared her head.

Outside, a storm raged.

Beyond her postage stamp window, snow blew horizontally. Though her father had spared no expense in the station's construction quality, the wind still howled. The whole pod shuddered with each gust.

"Good to go?" he asked.

She swallowed the knot of fear blocking her throat while tightening her grip on his hands. "I'm scared."

"Look at me . . ." He released her hands to cup her cheeks. "I can't make any promises, but I'll die before letting that crazy bastard hurt you again."

"That's just it," she said. "I don't want you hurt. You have to understand that when I broke up with you, it was because—"

"Don't stop on my account." Leo stood in the open door, flanked by three of his men who held mean-looking automatic rifles. "I'm a sucker for romance."

Heat drained from Eden's cheeks, pooling in her belly. "Leo, please . . . You're practically family. Why are you doing this?"

Sighing, stepping deeper into the room, he said, "I love you like a daughter—really, I do. I abhor violence. But I also cannot stand injustice, and what your father's kept from me for all these years is wrong. Criminal. The entire world deserves to know."

"I already told you, I don't have a clue what you're talking about."

"Liar." He raised his hand to slap her, but Jasper lunged between them, landing a hard right to Leo's face that resulted in blood spewing from his nose.

Two of Leo's henchman sprang into action, restraining Jasper by grabbing hold of his arms.

Jasper went slack, slipping from their hold, only to bolt back up swinging.

He got in a couple gut punches to the guy in front of him, but then the man behind him kneed him hard in the center of his lower back. The impact propelled Jasper forward. His attacker wrenched Jasper's arms back, slamming his face against the nearest wall.

Eden screamed, intent on getting to him. But before she'd moved more than a couple feet, one of Leo's men grabbed her, too, jerking her arms back to clasp her wrists.

While she fought for air, desperate to get to Jasper, Leo used the lap quilt at the foot of her bed to blot blood from his nose. Her mother had finished the quilt mere weeks before she'd died. For it to now be used as a rag turned Eden's stomach.

"That was a one-time mistake," Leo said to Jasper. To his men, he added, "I want those two loaded on the sub within the hour."

"Yessir."

The sub? Eden felt trapped in a nightmare from which she couldn't wake up. The station was her safe place. Leo had always been her friend. None of this made sense.

"Get the hell off me!" Jasper struggled to free himself, but was overpowered when two additional men entered, manhandling him back up against the wall. Yet another man appeared, jabbing a syringe into Jasper's upper arm. Jasper bucked and kicked to get free, but then faded. "I'll fucking *kiiillll . . .*" His sudden slur followed by silence terrified her.

"Did you kill him?" Eden escaped her captor's hold to rush to him, but now Leo held her back.

"Relax." Leo's voice was the same as it had always been, but all warmth was gone from his familiar blue gaze. "Why would I dream of hurting your sweetheart when he's more valuable to me as leverage than as a corpse?"

He nodded to the men holding Jasper upright. Gripping him under his arms, they dragged him out of her room and into the corridor.

Panic swirled her thoughts, but for Jasper's sake—her father's and Dane's too—she had to remain calm. She didn't have the luxury of falling apart.

"Leo, you're a scientist. Think about what you're doing. Where are my father and Dane? If you'd take me to them, I'm sure together we could figure this out."

"Later." He motioned to the lone mercenary standing beside him. "I prefer to deal with our friends after dinner. If you'd be so kind, Chad, please administer Eden's cocktail, then let's be on our way."

"Yessir." From a pocket on the right sleeve of his white parka, he withdrew another syringe. Before she had time to scream or even think, he'd plunged the contents into her arm.

Seconds later, Eden's world faded to black.

4

Jasper was initally slow to wake, but once consciousness was within reach, he fought for it. The day's events rushed at him like an angry wind.

Eden. Where was she? Was she all right?

He turned his head and found her beside him. She was out cold and like him, had her arms bound with zip ties. The faint rise and fall of her chest told him she was alive. Relief slowed his pulse.

Judging by their jostling surroundings, they'd been stashed in a moving snowcat's cargo hold. Angry rock music played over the howling wind. The two assholes who'd nailed him rode in front. Outside the vehicle's thick windows, they traveled through whiteout conditions. This time of year, the sun never set, which meant without the watch they'd taken from him, he had no basis for even guessing how long he'd been out. Why couldn't these guys have gone old school with a nice chloroform soaked rag? He could have detected the cloying sweetness and held his breath.

The driver said, "We should've been there by now. Check it again."

Jasper tensed while eavesdropping on the conversation.

"Already told you, GPS is offline. Satellite angle must be wrong."

"*Fuck.*" Judging by a loud thump, Jasper guessed the driver slammed the heel of his hand against the wheel. "I'm sick of this frozen nightmare. Nothing works. Ask me, Leo's lost his shit. There's no treasure—just some crazy, paranoid psycho chasing ghosts."

"Don't kill the messenger, man. Trust me, no one's more ready to get the hell out of here than I am. I've got a cousin in Hollywood who's gonna get me on with a stunt crew."

"Cool story, bro." That smart-assed comment ended the exchange.

Jasper raised his wrists to his mouth, pulling the zip tie mechanism as tight as it would go. From there, he lifted his arms over his head, then brought them down fast like a pair of chicken wings. The tie snapped.

Between the music and wind, his captors never

heard a thing.

It was no big surprise that the pocketknife he'd stashed in a front pocket was gone, which meant moving on to Plan B for freeing Eden.

The vehicle's layout served as a blessing. A high back bench seat hid most of the cargo area from casual view. Jasper used this fact to his advantage, rifling through the stacks of supplies and boxes until he found a large, hard plastic case loaded with weapons—everything from AK-47s to AR rifles to dozens of handguns and even a sweet RPG-7 shoulder rocket launcher. A second case held ammo. What were these guys anticipating? This amount of firepower struck him as serious overkill for over-throwing a scientific station on a continent where weapons of any kind were not allowed.

There were food stores and jugs of water. Vod-ka and candy wrapped in an unreadable language—German if he had to guess. Sleeping bags, tents and a camp stove. Ice cleats, ropes and climbing gear. Whoever these guys were, they'd packed enough goodies to stay a while. But again—why? If their plan was to take over the station, mission accom-plished. Why bring along an arsenal and an entire sporting goods store? Basic survival gear was a must in any situation, but this was overkill. There was even an array of head-mounted LED lights with dozens of back-up batteries.

Jasper glanced at Eden. Her chest rose and fell

steadily, but she was still out cold.

The loud rock music blared on and the two goons up front seemed unaware of his movements, so he went on to the last box.

Yahtzee. Not only was it loaded with the motherlode of first aid supplies and pill bottles ranging from antibiotics to painkillers, but there was also a zippered case holding prefilled syringes labeled Etorphine. Otherwise known as M99, it was an illegal opiate strong enough to bring down a freaking elephant. No wonder it had worked so fast on him and Eden.

They were damned lucky they weren't dead.

Filled with rage for what these idiots had done, Jasper helped himself to a pair of syringes, then belly crawled behind the bench seat. He removed the plastic safety tips, then slowly rose to administer both doses simultaneously.

Fury held his pulse and hands steady as he clenched the twin *weapons*, placing his thumbs on the smooth flat plungers.

"Sweet dreams, assholes . . ." He jabbed the syringes into their necks, then hopped over the seat to open the driver's door and shove him from the still moving vehicle. After also dispensing with the driver's friend by pushing him out the passenger-side door, Jasper stopped the rig long enough to kill the pounding music, then climb back over the seat to get to Eden.

"Hey, gorgeous . . ." He slipped his arm beneath her shoulders and gave her a light shake. "I sure could use some company. Mind waking up for me?"

Nothing.

His stomach knotted in fear.

After hefting her limp form over the seat back to rest on the front seat, he found a mummy-style sleeping bag to place over her, then realized they had big trouble. Leo's goons had chucked them into the snowcat's cargo hold wearing nothing but T-shirts, jeans and socks. If the vehicle broke down, they'd last mere minutes.

Thankfully, Leo's men had stashed their white parkas in back, so at least Jasper and Eden had those. He also found hats, face masks and gloves. The gear would swamp Eden, but this was about survival. Not fashion.

Unfortunately, getting boots wouldn't be so easy. His only option would be taking them from the human popsicles he'd dumped outside.

While foraging through one of the food bins, he remembered seeing protein bars stored in Ziploc bags. He found them, dumped the contents into the bin, and then slipped the bags over his feet. If he failed to locate at least one of the guys in a hurry, he'd be screwed.

He dressed in the available gear, then exited the vehicle out the rear cargo door.

Wind raged against him, making it tough to

even stand.

He squinted into the gloom for the men, but visibility was limited to about two feet in front of his face. He'd heard about guys dying in whiteout situations only to be found the next morning a few feet from their shelter. The stories were chilling. The reality provided a much-needed gut check.

He turned back to the cat for rope. He tied one end around his waist. The other end, to the door handle.

By this time, he'd dicked around long enough that his feet stung. A thousand tiny pinpricks made each step agony.

Blowing snow burned his cheeks with cold fire.

He trudged as far as the rope allowed, then fanned out until damn near falling over a body. Beyond relieved, he made fast work of removing the sorry bastard's boots, then yanking off the plastic bags to shove his own feet into fleece-lined footwear heaven. The Sorel's were so well-insulated they were still warm.

The fit was snug, but Jasper wasn't complaining.

He repeated the search pattern on the vehicle's opposite side until finding the other guy's boots for Eden.

Considering how many students and scientists these guys shared in killing, Jasper regretted giving them the luxury of meeting death in their sleep.

Back behind the wheel, Jasper checked Eden to

find her still out, but her breathing was regular.

Aiming one heater vent at her and the other at his face, he allowed himself a few minutes to thaw. He'd been in a lot of bad spots, but none that he could recall where literally, the air killed. As cold as it was outside, they might as well be on the moon. The climate was that inhospitable.

He needed to push forward, putting more distance between them and Leo's crew, but where was he supposed to go?

With the cat's cab silent, wind howled beyond the safety of metal and glass. That safety was an illusion. Who needed bad guys when Mother Nature had turned into a frigid bitch?

He reached for the dash-mounted GPS, but when he punched in McMurdo's coordinates, all he got was a message reading: *System Error*.

Frustration didn't begin to cover his dour mood.

He'd come down here expecting to encounter a lovable nerd herd. He'd expected Eden's cryptic message to be about a petri dish massacre. During hours and hours of travel, he'd fantasized about wild, buck-naked bunkbed, make-up sex. This was supposed to have been a seriously good time, yet so far Antarctica sucked.

For Jasper's entire military career, he'd been trained to embrace the suck, but honestly? He was tired.

He eased the cat into gear, then turned at a

ninety-degree angle from their previous course. In whiteout conditions, it was risky to move at all, yet he didn't feel comfortable returning to the station. He sure as hell didn't want to end up facing Leo's sub, but rolling off a cliff didn't sound that great, either.

He checked the fuel and found the tank three-quarters full.

A cat this size probably had a range of at least a few hundred miles. What would be helpful to know was the size of the storm. How close were they to the back edge?

With unlimited daylight, Jasper planned to drive at least another hour, then stop to rest and make a proper meal.

The vehicle's former occupants had been courteous enough to leave an iPhone attached to the stereo, so he slowed to glance through the playlists.

"What sounds good, gorgeous?" A hopeful glance in Eden's direction netted nothing but disappointment.

Wake up, babe. We've got a lot of unfinished business to go over. What we shared was real. You had to have felt it, too, right?

Even if she had, what gave him the right to act on those feelings? He couldn't hide out in Antarctica forever, and he sure as hell couldn't live with himself for ignoring his promise. The night his brother lost his wife, Jasper had sworn he'd never allow himself to even think about falling in love.

Shaking his head as if that would help erase the memory of the awful night Mariah had died, Jasper focused on the here and now. Music. Something peaceful to wake Eden.

"Let's see . . . We have playlists called—and I'm not kidding: *Weight-lifting, Screwing, Driving, Gun Range,* and one far too vile for your tender ears." Hoping for the best, Jasper picked the second.

Then all hell broke loose to the soothing strains of Marvin Gaye crooning, *"Let's Get it On."*

Bam. The cat struck rock.

The impact jolted Jasper forward and then back. He shot his arm out protectively to brace Eden.

With the vehicle slanted at an unnavigable angle, the tracks lurched, then groaned while gliding back.

The motor chugged, coughed, then died.

Helping himself to what remained of the precious battery power, Marvin kept right on singing above the wind's eerie howl.

Jasper killed the music.

How long would they have before the bone-chilling temp killed them?

5

Eden winced, cupping her gloved hands over her eyes to shield them from the painful glare of sun against snow.

Confused didn't begin to cover how she felt; her head ached and grogginess left her disoriented, but then she saw Jasper and the nightmare with Leo came roaring back.

"Good morning," Jasper said from a few feet away. He sat cross-legged alongside a camp stove, stirring what looked and smelled like scrambled eggs. She spied an open package of a freeze-dried breakfast complete with peppers, potatoes and cheese.

Coffee also flavored the frigid air.

"Hey." Her stomach rumbled. "Mind letting me

in on what happened? I mean, I remember the showdown with Leo and his thugs, but—" she shivered despite wearing full outdoor gear and being inside a sleeping bag "—how did we get from there to what I'm guessing is a crashed snowcat?"

"Funny story," he said with the crooked grin she'd fallen for the first time they'd met at *Tattered Cover*, her favorite Denver bookstore. It had been snowing, and he had been nursing a hot chocolate while searching for the latest Martha Stewart cookbook for his landlord. Here was this big, strong guy oblivious to his adorable whipped cream mustache. She'd fallen fast and hard. She'd helped him find the book, then cancelled that afternoon's office hours at the small college where she taught English Lit. The rest of the day was spent talking and laughing and kissing and eventually tumbling into bed. She'd never gone that fast with a man—before or since. But Jasper did things to her heart and mind and body that she still didn't fully understand. And now, thanks to her diagnosis, she never would. "Those two Neanderthals who nailed us? I had the pleasure of returning the favor. I figured from there we were home free. All I had to do was drive a ways before riding out the storm, but then a big pile of rocks attacked us, and *wham*. We're kinda stuck."

"The rocks attacked us?" She cocked her right eyebrow.

"It was bad, babe. Glad you weren't awake to

witness the carnage." He turned off the stove to cross the short distance to kiss her. Lord help her, she let him. His lips were at first cold, but then warmed with their combined heat. She groaned when he offered a sweep of his tongue. "Mmm . . . I missed you. Let's for sure have more of that in a bit. But first, let's get this food in you before it gets cold."

He handed her a fork and they both ate from the pan.

"Almost forgot," he said between bites. "I made instant coffee." He reached next to the stove for a tall, stainless steel covered mug. "It's not exactly a Starbucks, and no cream or sugar, but it's hot."

"That works for me. Thanks." The soothing drink and food heated her from the inside out. They were lucky to have it. "Don't suppose you've seen any pee funnels? Going in the snow is frowned upon."

He winced. "Afraid not. Leo's crew wasn't especially environmentally friendly. Hold on a sec, and I'll at least make you pee bucket." He dumped gear from a five-gallon model, and even found her a pack of wet wipes. "I'll head outside. Knock on the glass when you're done."

Never had she wished more for tinted windows.

Finished, she had no choice but to dump it in the snow, which was seriously uncool. She buried it, but still felt awful.

A few minutes later, once they were both back inside, Jasper asked, "Want the good news? Or the bad, or the *really* bad?"

She groaned. "After yesterday, I'm kind of at my bad news max."

"Ditto." He leaned in for another kiss she should have pushed away from, but couldn't. She needed him—his strength. Just for a little while. Then she'd let him go. "But you need to know where things stand. I climbed to the top of the rock pile we ran into, and got the GPS to pick up a signal. As the crow flies, we're a couple hundred miles from McMurdo. No biggee if the crash hadn't killed the engine."

"I'm assuming you couldn't see in the white-out?"

"True, but still . . ." He hardened his jaw. "I've landed us in a helluva jam."

"Stop. If it weren't for you, we probably wouldn't even be alive. I still can't believe that for all these years, a monster has been lurking inside Leo. How could he have killed so many people? And for what? There's no treasure. The whole idea is silly. Which makes what he did all the more senseless." Needing comfort, she fished out the locket she'd worn since her father gave it to her on her twelfth birthday. Just rubbing the family tree etching brought her strength. As did touching the amethyst birthstone at the tree's roots. "And where are my father and Dane? Did Leo hurt them, too?"

"Wish I knew." He sat beside her, and she rested her head against his shoulder. Even through bulky winter gear, her body sang to be near him. At the moment, the song was tragic but welcome all the same. "Back to our options, I'm no MacGyver when it comes to engine repairs, but now that the wind's died down enough for me to see my hand in front of my face, I'll do my damnedest to get this thing back on a flat angle and running. We'd have warmth and plenty of gear—maybe even enough fuel. But the real kicker is all of this . . ." He gestured out the window toward a sea of endless white punctuated by imposing Mount Erebus. "If we have such great visibility, so does Leo. I hope he was lying about his sub and having even more manpower. If he wasn't, that means he could already be looking for us, and in this red cat, we'll be an easy target to find. I'd say we could at least monitor his movements with our *friends'* radio, but it's dead."

"So what do we do? Set out on foot? Try making it back to our station for snowmobiles?"

"That's an option. But what if Crazy Leo did fabricate the whole sub thing and he's really just hanging out in his lab, waiting for his next victims?"

She sighed.

"On the flip side," Jasper said, "I have a hard time buying the fact that Leo doesn't have some basis for launching his treasure hunt. There's thousands of dollars in gear and weapons in this vehicle alone. There's no telling what else he may have. A guy doesn't stock up like this on a lark, you know? Think, Eden. Has your dad or this Dane guy you've been talking about ever even hinted at there being more going on down here than standard research?"

Rubbing her temples, she said, "Honestly, all of their work is so complex. When they talk about it, I glaze over. I know Dad's trying to cure cancer, and he's had promising leads, but—"

"Didn't your mom die of ovarian cancer?"

Eden nodded.

"So up until her death, he was driven by a desire to save her?"

"I guess so."

"This is a longshot, but could this treasure be a pharmaceutical thing? There's huge money in drugs. What if your dad and Dane discovered a formula or new bio-organism that's a scientific game changer and Leo wants it?"

"They were partners. They worked together for years. My father isn't a selfish man. Every dime he's ever made either went to my mother's medical bills, my education, or the station and his studies." Because Eden couldn't bear for her father to sink still more money and hopes into her losing cause, she hadn't even told him about her prognosis. What was the point? She'd had a front row seat to her mother's physical and emotional breakdown, and the harder she'd fought, the worse the physical toll had been. Eden wanted no part of that. When it was her time, she'd accept it gracefully. Until then, she needed to regain her composure and help ensure Jasper reached safety. Her life was already gone, but she'd fight for his and her father's. "When the first of the students were shot, I wanted to find my father and Dane, but you can't imagine the chaos. All I could do was hide, but like I told you, one of Leo's men easily found me. It was . . ." Cold enveloped her from the inside out. She used to love this place. The isolation. The pure, unspoiled beauty. Now, she'd give anything to be far away from here, in a place where if she tipped her face to the sun, warm rays would soak in like a healing balm. Like Jasper's softest caress. "Aside from watching my mother die, it was the hardest thing I've ever done—hiding like a coward beneath a table. I should have fought back."

"Give yourself credit for staying alive." He kissed the crown of her head. "You pretty sure your dad and Dane made it out alive?"

"Yes." *I hope.* "Unless Leo caught them later and . . ." She couldn't bring herself to finish the sentence.

"Could they have gone to McMurdo for help?"

"I suppose? But if they had, wouldn't help have already arrived? I was alone with Leo a few days before you arrived. Doug plays online chess with my dad. He would have mentioned him being at

McMurdo. But now, he's probably dead, too." She shivered. "What are we going to do?"

"Since it's cold as balls in here—" he formed a smoke ring with his foggy breath "—I vote we're proactive. I'll try getting the engine started. You make a proper inventory of our food. In this cold, we ideally need about six thousand calories per day. Give me a guesstimate of how many days we've got at say six, four, or two thousand a day. We might find civilization in hours. If not, we need to be prepared."

"Agreed."

He opened the cat's rear door and leaped out.

The even deeper cold hit her face like a slap.

"Jasper!" she called.

"Yeah?" He squinted against the sun, then took sunglasses from a pocket on his coat and slipped them on.

"Are we going to be okay?"

"Absolutely. All you need to worry about is getting back to civilization. Because once we're in a toasty coffee house, I fully intend to make you explain what you were thinking when you dumped a great catch like me." His toothy grin and wink started a flutter low in her belly.

In light of their circumstances, she had no business thinking about anything other than getting help to find her father, but Jasper had always had a way about him that brightened the darkest corner.

She fought to find a smile, but nodded instead. Yes, she needed to tell him exactly what she'd been thinking when she'd broken her own heart by breaking up with him, but this was neither the time nor place.

With him outside, she did as he asked, counting an assortment of freeze-dried meals, MREs, and four cases of protein bars that held a hundred forty-four bars each. While it was a relief to know running short on food wouldn't be their most pressing issue, that fact did little to hold fear at bay. He'd asked her to run specific calorie computations, but in the cold there was no way she could hold her focus long enough to run the figures in her head.

She found more sunglasses on the dash, then stared out the window at the stark view that usually brought solace.

Now, the desolation raised her pulse. They were in a bad spot, but if anyone could get them out, it would be Jasper.

From outside the vehicle came a few clangs, then curses.

She'd cleaned their breakfast pan as best she could with snow, and was contemplating boiling water for the cocoa packets she'd found when Jasper yanked open the front door to try the engine.

Fingers crossed, she held her breath while awaiting the results.

The engine turned three times, but didn't start.

He cursed under his breath, then headed back outside.

What if the fix was too complex to manage in the field? It happened all the time. Usually, operators radioed for help and it proved no big deal. In their case, everything was a big deal.

She hopped out of the cab to join him. "Anything I can do?"

"No, thanks. Get back inside, so you're at least out of the wind." Though it was nowhere near the speed that had induced yesterday's whiteout conditions, it was still brisk.

"Jasper, please. I want to help."

"Then get inside, so I don't have to worry about you and the engine."

While his brusque demeanor didn't exactly fill her with warm fuzzies, she'd been around enough guys at the station to understand that for most, working on engines wasn't anyone's favorite chore.

Trying not to take his anger personally, she climbed back into the vehicle to start the camp stove. Jasper loved cocoa. He'd probably never admit it to the tough-guy former SEALs he worked with, but he especially enjoyed mini-marshmallows on top. Grinning at the naughty memory of what they'd once done with the tasty morsels, her cheeks overheated.

She lurched in surprise when the driver's-side door opened and Jasper gave the ignition another try.

Ruh, ruh, ruh.

More cursing.

"I'm making hot chocolate," she said. "Want some?"

"No. What I want is for this stupid-ass engine to start. I've checked the hydraulic lines and plugs—everything looks good."

"I don't mean to get in your man-business, but I was out with a team a few years back, and we got stuck in a blizzard. The cat crapped out on us, and to make a long, cold story short—I remember this, because while shivering, a friend and I were joking about craving warm carbs like cookies and brownies, when—"

"I'm freezing. Could you please get to the punchline?"

"Stop being snippy. I'm trying to help."

"I know, babe. Sorry. But the longer we sit here, the more time Leo has to find us. Or, we could just turn into human popsicles. Neither scenario holds much appeal."

"Okay, well, my friend and I were joking about carbs, but our driver checked the carburetor and found a ring of frost around some thingamajig. Started with a V. Ventricle? Venus? Sorry—can't remember."

"Venturi?"

"Maybe? I really don't know. My friend was on

engagement-ring watch, so we'd turned the ring of frost into dreaming of diamond rings."

"Right." He sharply exhaled before heading back outside, slamming the door behind him.

She'd never seen his cranky side and didn't especially like it.

But then this was also their first life-threatening experience.

How would he take the news that she was essentially a dead woman walking? Oddly enough, she'd made her peace with it. It was easier. There was no sense dwelling on what was to come. And she sure wouldn't spend whatever time she had left hugging a commode. Her poor mother had been sick to the extreme. A bag of bones, clinging to life for her little girl and husband. By the end, Eden had been glad to see her go, because she could no longer bear witnessing the constant pain in her eyes.

Eden used the backs of her gloves to blot tears from her eyes before they froze, then swallowed the knot in throat. The here and now was all that mattered, so she returned to the pleasantly mundane task of lighting the propane camp stove, then retrieving snow to thaw and boil.

By the time she'd made two mugs of hot chocolate, Jasper was once again tugging open the door, then easing behind the wheel.

She crossed her fingers.

Ruh, ruh. Ruh, ruh.

He slapped the palm of his gloved hand against the wheel, then tried one last time. *Ruh, ruh, rrrruh . . ."*

Eden dared exhale when the engine finally caught, then settled into a comforting chug.

"*Yes . . .*" Jasper grinned over his shoulder, turned on the heater, then directed all vents in her direction. "You're amazing." He blew her a kiss. "I never would have thought to check the carb, but sure enough, whether it was caused by the blowing snow or the impact when I hit the rocks, there was a ring of ice. Once I got it cleared—voila."

"Glad I could finally help." She was beginning to feel her assigned tasks were busy work. After climbing over the gear, she handed him his reward. "Drink up. You're probably freezing."

He drank, then closed his eyes and groaned. "You're an angel. Thanks." He took a few more sips. "How are we on food?"

"I didn't do the actual math, but there's plenty. If our gas holds out, more than enough to get us to McMurdo. But then you probably already knew that."

"Maybe." He winked. "I had to do something to get your mind off of the very real possibility of freezing to death."

The heater had kicked into high gear. She could have purred in relief.

"Let's get the stove and any loose supplies secured, then head out."

"Aye, aye, captain." She gave him a saucy salute.

Before coaxing the massive machine down from its awkward angle, he grinned and shook his head. "I always loved that about you."

"What?"

"How you make bad situations good. Remember that time we spent an hour shopping for our Cinco de Mayo feast, only to get to the checkout to discover—"

"Neither of us had our wallets." She'd finished his sentence. Of course she remembered. Every moment they'd ever shared. Good or bad, she cherished all of their time together.

"After getting back to your place, didn't we order Chinese?"

"Yeah, and you dropped sweet and sour sauce all over the carpet. There's still a stain."

"Sorry." With the cat on flat ground and chugging toward safety, he leaned close enough to kiss her cheek. "Once we get out of this mess, I'll replace it."

"Thanks, but not necessary." She cast him a sad, slow-fading smile.

"Why'd you do it, babe?"

She hung her head.

"Don't play dumb. You know exactly what I'm talking about. Sure, I had my own issues and shouldn't have taken things much further, but I was working through them. Given time, they might have been resolved. But when you cut me off cold . . ." A muscle twitched in his jaw. "That hurt. Why'd you break up with me? Did I do something to offend you? Were you that pissed about the carpet?"

"No. Please just know it wouldn't have worked between us. You would have only ended up getting hurt, so I had to let you go."

"That's such BS." He glanced in her direction. "We've got hours to hash this out, so let's get on with it. Why, when we were beyond perfect together, did you suddenly dump me?"

6

"Because I'm sick, okay?"

"What do you mean? Like *bad* sick?" Jasper's stomach tightened—not the way it did when dodging bullets, but on a deeper, more profound level. Like the kind he'd experienced after what happened to Kyle's wife. He'd expected Eden to say he was too messy or worked too much or cussed too much or did any of the annoying things he no doubt did on a daily basis. He'd even steeled himself for the possibility that she'd found another man. Never had he seen anything like this coming.

The cab had grown warm enough for Eden to remove her gloves.

Jasper watched while she primly set them on her lap, then covered her face with her hands.

"Answer me." Too hot, he unzipped his coat, and shrugged free of it before pitching it over the bench seat. "I have a right to know."

"Okay . . ." Silvery tears trailed down her cheeks, glinting in the too-bright sun. "Right after you were assigned to guard the governor, I went to my annual physical. Everything seemed fine until the test results came in showing that I'm not—fine. Just like my mom, I have ovarian cancer. Yay, me—it runs in families."

"What happened next? I'm assuming you went to a specialist?"

She nodded. "He wanted me to have surgery right away. Start treatments. Yada, yada."

"Did you?"

"No. What's the point? I watched Mom go through all of that, and for what? She died anyway. She was miserable—throwing up for hour-long stretches at a time. I was ten. Watching my father sit next to her alongside the toilet, holding back the long hair of the wig she'd insisted on wearing ever since I'd opened my big mouth to say she looked scary with no hair."

Jasper stopped the cat.

His next move was to reach for Eden, sliding her across the vinyl seat and onto his lap. She was crying, only they weren't ordinary tears. Though he had no way of knowing, he got the impression he was holding the grief-stricken little girl who still missed her mom. While he ached for her, he also needed to get through to the adult Eden. He needed to make her understand that just because her mother's story had a shitty ending, that didn't mean hers would, too.

"So . . ." He rested his chin atop her head. "You hit the pause button on you and me, because you assume you're about to die?"

"We're not paused," she said against his chest. "We're done. I saw what my dad went through, and there's no way I'm putting you through that. It's not fair."

"Oh—" his short laugh was anything but funny "—let me get this straight. It's perfectly cool for you to deal with fucking cancer on your own?"

"Shut up. I made my decision. There's nothing you can do to change my mind."

"The hell there's not. For starters, as soon as we get off this ice cube of a continent, you're going back to that specialist and scheduling surgery, and as many treatments as it takes to heal you."

"You're being ridiculous. If it were that easy, don't you think I'd have tried? What don't you understand about the fact that I want to die on my terms? I want to go out gracefully and at peace."

He hardened his jaw. "What don't you understand about the fact that I refuse to let you die?"

"This is cancer." She backed away. "Not some gun-toting terrorist you can eradicate with a smart bomb. This enemy isn't beatable by sheer will."

"The hell it isn't." After putting the cat back in gear, he continued their forward momentum. "And you and me? We're officially back together."

"No."

"Not up for debate."

"Exactly. There's nothing to even discuss. We're done."

"You're being ridiculously short-sighted. And selfish."

"*Selfish?*" she shrieked. "Screw you."

"Oh, hell . . . Seriously? Now?" Looked like their lover's tiff would have to be tabled.

"What are you talking about?" She glanced up, only to groan. On the horizon loomed three snow-cats—each double the size of their own. "I don't recognize those. Could they be part of Leo's crew? What are we going to do?"

"This . . ." Jasper maneuvered their gangly vehicle into a U-turn, then aimed toward the mountain range they'd spent most of the morning veering away from. "How well do you know this area?"

"Not at all. Aside from a few student field outings, I haven't been this far from the station since Mom died." She glanced out the rear window. "They're gaining. I guess this means Leo wasn't lying. About his additional manpower. Maybe even the sub."

"I still think the whole treasure thing is pharmaceutical. Your dad must be onto something big, and Leo doesn't just want a piece of the pie, but the whole, damned thing."

"But if that were the case, why bother with me? What information could I have that he needs? I definitely didn't inherit the science gene from my father."

A quick look in the rearview did zero to squash the growing hum of frustration in Jasper's head. Learning about Eden's cancer was enough for one day. Though he hadn't wanted to mention it to her, Jasper figured their path would eventually cross with that of Leo and crew, but he hadn't expected it to happen this soon.

There was a shitload of firepower in the back, but if the two losers he'd offed had that obscene amount, how much would Leo's main crew have? Meaning him and Eden were hopelessly outgunned.

"On this plain, there's nowhere to hide." They rode along the center of a wide valley lined by foothills and then peaks. "Look for an opening where we can veer off. We might even get lucky and have a wind whip up the snow, hiding us—and our tracks—from view."

"See where those two hills seem to overlap?" She pointed to an area maybe three miles away. The light was different here—the air too clear. Judging distance was nearly impossible.

"Good job. I like it." Even if he hadn't, it wasn't

like they had much of a choice. He gunned the engine for all it was worth, getting a couple extra miles-per-hour. Would it make a difference? Probably not. But for Eden's sake, he had to try.

The cat shuddered from the pace, but held up long enough to enter the snowy canyon's mouth well ahead of Leo's contingency. The trouble was that with such clear visibility, there was no such thing as hiding. Not only would Leo have seen where they turned, but the tracks stood out as if they'd been spray painted blaze orange.

Perpetual winds had topped the canyon's jagged walls with freeform towers of ice and snow. They were beautiful, but delicately balanced. What would it take to bring them down?

Steering the cat beneath them didn't do much for his nerves, but then an idea struck. "Have any idea how long this canyon is?"

"Sorry, no. It could wind on for miles or end around the bend."

Clenching the wheel, he craned to view the snow towers from a fresh angle. Would it be enough? He had no choice but to try.

Stopping, he killed the engine to save fuel.

"What are you doing?" she asked. "We have to keep going."

"You saw how Leo was gaining. See the snow up there?"

She nodded. "It's beautiful. Ice towers that large

might have taken a decade to form—maybe a century."

"My apologies to Mother Nature," he said as he climbed over the seat to reach the weapons cache. Finally, something that made him feel at home. The guys at Trident would be jealous when they heard about his new toy. He dug out the RPG-7, then grabbed a few rockets before leaving the cat.

"Are you crazy?" Eden shouted after him. "You can't fire that in this canyon. This entire continent is protected. The damage may never be repaired."

"I'm real sorry, but at the moment that can't be helped." Leaving the rear door open, he set spare ammo on a food bin, then loaded and prepared to fire. "Cover your ears," he shouted when the low rumble of Leo's cats could be heard.

"If you have to play with explosives, why not just shoot the vehicles?"

"Because they no doubt have even better toys than we do, which means by the time I disabled one of their cat's they'd decimate ours."

"Oh." She tugged her gloves back on, then did as he'd asked.

Bam. He fired at the overhang nearest the canyon's mouth.

While his ears still rang from the first rocket's concussive force, then the rumble from the cascade of falling snow and ice, he fired at the canyon's opposite side, bringing down yet more ice and snow.

Yes. His plan worked—even better than expected. A thirty-foot wall of snow had fallen, closing the entry with a wide, frozen swath.

"Hate to be a Debbie Downer," Eden said from behind him, "but if Leo has a rocket launcher, too, what's to stop him from blowing through your pile?"

"Honestly? Not a damned thing. Let's get going." For good measure, once she'd climbed back into the vehicle, Jasper fired off two more rounds—this time at the rock walls. He didn't fool himself into believing his barricade was impenetrable, but it would hopefully buy them time.

He stowed the weapon, then climbed back behind the wheel.

Moments earlier, he'd been too warm, but now that the adrenaline had worn off, he shivered.

Even ten tense minutes later with the heat blasting, he couldn't get warm.

What the hell was he doing down here? He and Eden should be back in Denver, getting her treated.

A glance in her direction showed her grim-faced, holding her arms crossed defensively. The fact that neither had spoken a word after one of the most stressful binds he'd been in since his former SEAL days didn't bode well for their relationship. What was she thinking? Was she scared for her father? Worried about Leo's men breaking through the barrier? Pissed about him harming the environment? Why wasn't she talking? Why couldn't he think of anything comforting to say?

They jostled along the narrow canyon floor for a good couple hours when the unspoken fear he'd most dreaded when cutting off their exit became their new reality.

Not only was the route impassable with the cat, but even to climb out would require specialized climbing gear and expertise they didn't have. Back in Denver, his pal, Everett, got his weekend adrenaline dosage by free-climbing sheer cliff walls, but heights had never been Jasper's thing.

Steam vents and a boulder-field were dead ahead, reminding him that if the climate wasn't already forbidding enough, volcanoes stood by, ready to make life even more exciting.

"Now what?" Eden's question barely rose above the cat's steady chug.

"Not sure." Not only was there nowhere to go, but even if they'd wanted to bolt, their sole means of transport was perilously low on fuel. He kept that fact to himself. They had enough food to last weeks, but the cold could prove far more deadly than the crew they'd been trying to outrun.

"A few years ago, Dad took me and a few students to a steam vent that was near a small cave. Maybe these vents have one nearby. It might be warmer than the cat once it's out of fuel."

"You noticed we're getting low?"

"You thought I wouldn't?"

Staring straight ahead, he shrugged.

"I appreciate you trying to protect me from the realities of our situation, but I'm a big girl, Jasper. I can take it."

"You shouldn't have to. None of this makes sense. Even back to the dead orcas you found on the shore. What killed them? Why?"

The cab had grown overly warm. She'd removed her gloves and coat. Holding her fingers to her temples, she rubbed in a tight circle.

"Headache?"

"A little. I'm just trying to think of what could have happened to those whales. The penguins, too. It had to be something quick. I remember reading once about how military sonar has been linked to mass strandings and even deaths, but how would that apply here? There's no military presence in Antarctica."

As far as we know.

Jasper had worked in special ops long enough to know things weren't always what they seemed. "What I wouldn't give for ten minutes with my iPad to research fringe sonar usage. Just for grins and giggles, let's say there is a treasure. Could our buddy Leo actually have a sub that was searching the coast with ground penetrating sonar that killed the whales? Could it have been strong enough to have even caused a localized earthquake?"

"I guess? I mean, sure. At this point, anything's

possible, but even if there were a treasure—and that's a very big *if*—why all of the weapons? Why kill everyone at the station? Why keep only me alive?"

"Because somehow, you're connected to solving this mystery, and it might be bigger than we ever imagined. You asked earlier why Leo wouldn't have ordered his men to blast through the wall we made. For one simple reason—he can't risk hurting you. Whatever your dad has that Leo wants, you're the key."

"Gee . . ." She winced. "That makes me feel so much better."

"Sorry, but it's the truth. You're our one ace in a hand loaded with Jokers."

"Your stupid poker analogy isn't helping." Her faint smile belied her harsh words.

"You used to love a good game of strip poker . . ." He skimmed the backs of his fingers along her cheek. Her color heightened with his dirty innuendo. She was great in bed. They'd been great. Did she remember? He needed her to.

She placed her hand over his, capturing it, holding on tight. "I said I was okay with dying . . . But I lied. I'm scared, and all of this is only making my fear worse. My plan was to go out on my terms, but—"

"Stop." He brought her hand to his mouth, kissing the back, then turning it over to kiss her palm.

Her quickened breathing didn't escape him. She might say she was done with him, but that was a lie, just like the reassurances he felt obligated to spew. "You're going to be fine. We both are. Let's grab some gear, and hike our way out of here."

"You can't be serious? It's thirty below. Those rock walls are impenetrable, and even a mountain goat would have trouble navigating with the size of the rocks going forward. Supposing we do get out of this canyon, what if Leo and his men are waiting on the other side?"

"I've got another plan." He winked, then pointed out the window. "I'm not willing to surrender just yet. Those steam vents you said might be attached to a small cave? What if we go all in and hope for more—like if Leo's still coming for you, there's enough room to set up an ambush, then pick them off one-by-one. After that, we hike out to their cats and mosey our way back to McMurdo in time for movie night. It's possible, right?"

"Sure. I guess that could work. But . . ."

"That's all I need to know. Come on," he held out his hand. "Help me load our gear. We've got a lot to set up for this to go as planned."

"For the record, I think you're being ridiculously optimistic."

"Whatever. It's not like we've got anything better to do. Unless . . ." He squeezed her hand. "Are you feeling frisky?"

His hopeful wink earned him a playful smack. "You wish."

Yes, I do. Never had he been happier than when the two of them had been together. She'd soothed the beasts left in his mind and heart from five Gulf tours, and more covert missions into various hell-holes than he cared to remember. Most of all, she made him recall what it had been like to be uncondi-tionally loved when his own family no longer spoke to him. At least, he hoped she'd loved him. If not, maybe he had an even bigger problem.

At the rear of the cat, all decked out in their full arctic finery—he'd sliced the front seat to get pad-ding to make Eden's boots fit tighter—they stood side-by-side, appraising supplies. While all of it could be needed at one time or another, there was no way they could practically transport it for any ap-preciable distance. Which meant tough decisions had to be made.

Potentially life-saving decisions.

There were no backpacks, so after jogging back to the front for the GPS, Jasper rigged a cargo net into a bag that he crammed with freeze dried meals, drink packs, a compact jet-boil stove, an aluminum pan and two spoons and mugs.

For warmth, the two sleeping bags and tent were a must.

"Do me a favor," he said to Eden, pointing to-ward the first aid kit. "There are a couple of smaller kits in there that are loaded with bandages and other odds and ends. Dump those, and then refill them with an assortment of anything you think might be useful."

"That would be all of it . . ."

"Agreed, but if we can't carry it, it won't do us much good."

When it came to choosing the most practical weapon, he opted for a sheathed hunting knife and two 9mms that he fit into the waistband of his pants. "Can you shoot?"

"No. I've never even touched a gun."

"Time for you to learn." Not sure who or what they might encounter, he fit eight boxes of ammo into his coat pockets. Four hundred rounds seemed like more than enough, but the way their luck was running, who knew? "As soon as we get settled in the cave, you'll get your first lesson."

"Yay."

Ignoring her lack of enthusiasm, he fit elastic-banded LED headlamps over their hats, then crammed two spare units and batteries into her coat pockets.

"Do you think it's odd," he asked, "that our friends had all of this lighting gear when it won't be dark outside for months?"

"Very. Like they anticipated doing a little spe-lunking."

He slung long coils of banded rope over each

shoulder. "Ready?"

She grimaced.

"Perfect. Let's go." From their vantage point, the steam vents were maybe a couple hundred yards deeper into the increasingly more rugged canyon. Hiking with his awkward load sucked. Toss in the added weight and lack of mobility of the bulky winter gear, and each step felt like ten. He looked back to find Eden's lips pressed tight. "You all right?"

"Swell."

"Need me to carry something?"

She shook her head.

Twenty minutes later, the steam plumes still looked two hundred yards away. Nowhere in the world had he been such a crappy judge of distance. If Leo and his crew were following on foot, they had to be making better time.

He drove himself to a faster pace, but Eden struggled keeping up.

Slowing, he took the med kit from her, as well as the batteries.

"I said I can do it," she complained.

"There's no doubt in my mind you can, but maybe I think you shouldn't have to."

She rolled her eyes before snatching back the med kit, then plowing ahead.

That's my girl. He couldn't help but be proud of her spunk. But if she had this much of a competitive spirit in taking a damned walk, why didn't she feel the same about defeating cancer?

Forty minutes worth of scrambling over rocks and boulders netted not much of anything special. No cave. No hot spring perfect for skinny-dipping. Nothing but the lone steam vent, plus more rocks and snow and ice capped by cheery blue sky.

A glance at his watch that he'd found stashed with the gear showed it was ten at night.

No wonder he was so freaking tired.

Through a particularly rough patch, she asked, "What if Leo's not following us? What if we've done all of this for nothing? And his goal was to drive us into the wild to let nature do his dirty work?"

"Not gonna lie . . ." He paused to stretch his back. "It's a possibility."

His grand plan had been to set up for an ambush, but now they were back on an open plain that more closely resembled the moon than any image he'd imagined of Antarctica. Where were the happy penguins and tourist cruises?

"See that overhang?" He pointed north—at least what he thought was north. He felt all turned around and embarrassed by his lackluster navigation skills.

"Yeah. It might as well be a million miles from here."

"Nah. Only a half-mil."

She flipped him off, only her bulky glove stole

her thunder.

"You're sexy when you're mad."

"Stow it."

"Say the word, and you know I'll—"

"Shh." She looked to the sky. "Hear that?"

"The sound of my heart breaking from your rejection?"

"No, listen . . ."

No way. "Is that a . . ."

A helicopter banked low and to the right, hammering them with brutally cold wind.

Jasper pulled Eden close, shielding her from the worst of the blow.

The craft hovered. The cargo door opened and two men dressed all in white save for mirror-lensed sunglasses dropped a rope, then slid down it.

Eight more guys followed.

Through the craft's open side door, a struggle broke out between one last man dressed all in white and another who wore a familiar red civilian coat. A ladder was tossed out.

The guy in red hesitated before he was shoved from the hovering craft, forced to climb down at gunpoint.

"Recognize him?" Jasper shouted above the rhythmic thump.

"I-I think that's my father's friend Dane."

7

The chopper's wake sliced Eden's cheeks like invisible razors. She gladly stepped into Jasper's outstretched arms, but then realized hiding wouldn't make the bad guys go away—or rescue Dane.

"Give me my gun!" she shouted over the chopper's roar.

"You don't know how to shoot!"

"No time like the present to learn! We have to save him!"

Jasper dropped the gear to take two menacing handguns from his waistband.

While the bad guys huddled, then coaxed Dane forward by pressing the barrel of an M-16 into his back, Jasper handed her a weapon. "Hold it like this." He positioned her right hand around the grip, and her left on top of the slide. "Pull back to chamber the first load, then do the deed."

"I'm not sure I can kill anyone."

Jasper fired off several rounds before shots pinged off the rock beside her.

She growled, then spun around with a roar, matching Jasper's every round. She hadn't hit anyone yet, but with the chopper gone, the bad guys scattered, dodging behind boulders, only ducking out to take potshots. Her pulse went haywire with terror.

She'd lost sight of Dane. Had he been hurt?

"Run for higher ground," Jasper said beside her. "I'll cover and look for your dad's friend."

"What about you?"

"I can take care of myself. Go!"

Eden ran for all she was worth—terror fueling her legs. She took cover behind the nearest boulder, then fired five times until her gun stopped working.

"What's wrong with it?" she asked once Jasper joined her.

"Probably jammed. Let me have it." He pulled the slider back, and a bullet casing popped out. He fired, then dropped the cartridge from the handle, counting her remaining ammo before slamming it back in. He returned the gun to her. "See that ridge?" He pointed to a rocky outcropping above them. "Head up and over that spot. You'll be safe from the line of fire."

"Come with me."

"I'm good. You've got nine shots left, so make them count. I'll reload you as soon as soon as we meet up."

"But—"

"Quit arguing, and go." He kissed her forehead, then nudged her in the direction he'd pointed.

With every shot fired, she flinched. So much for Jasper's theory about Leo not wanting her hurt. To catch her breath, she ducked behind a towering boulder, only to burst into happy tears.

Her dad's business partner, the man who had been like a second father to her ever since her mother died, stood before her, holding out his arms.

"Dane. You're okay." She ran to him, hugging him as tight as her oversized coat allowed.

"Likewise." He was out of breath. "Your father and I have been out of our minds worrying about you."

"You've seen him? He's okay?"

"He was this morning. Or was that yesterday morning? Leo and his men have me all confused."

"No kidding, right? Leo's crazy. What happened?"

"I don't know, love. He snapped."

"Do you know anything about a hidden treasure?"

He shook his head.

"Eden, I told you to—oh." Jasper froze.

"Jasper." She pulled him into their shelter. "This

is Dane. He saw my dad yesterday."

"Where?" Jasper asked.

"In a sub of all places. Leo has interesting friends. Turns out for years he's been part of an incredibly well-funded Neo-Nazi group who call themselves the *True Reich*."

"What are you doing here?" Jasper's gaze narrowed. "Why did they force you from the chopper?"

Eden didn't like Jasper's distrustful tone. "Can't you tell Leo's men took him, too? He was trying to run away, weren't you, Dane?"

"Yes." Dane shuddered before working up a faint smile. "Exactly."

Jasper's gaze narrowed. "And out of all of Antarctica, you just happened to run here? Right where we were hiding?"

"No, you don't understand. Leo's men have been following you. Eden, Leo told me you were with a friend. When your father escaped, they brought me here to talk with both of you. Leo wants me to try getting Eden to spill whatever she knows about this supposed treasure he believes is linked to a conspiracy theory about Hitler having constructed an underground compound. I told him that even as your father's closest friend, I had never heard such a farfetched, outlandish claim, but Leo insists the treasure is real."

"Whether it is or isn't," Jasper said, "the bullets those guys have been shooting are very real. Let's table this discussion, then get over that ridge." He nodded toward the spot where he'd previously asked her to go.

"I've got a better idea." Dane left the rock's cover, emerging with his hands up. "Gentlemen!" he called to the shooters. "Please, hold your fire! I've found Carl's daughter, and she's agreed to go with us peaceably."

"The hell she did," Jasper mumbled.

Eden elbowed him. "Hush. I'm sure Dane knows what he's doing."

"Unless he's planning to get us all killed. I don't like it. I'm not going anywhere with those guys, and neither are you."

"I'm unarmed." Dane steadily moved closer. "Please, call back the chopper and we'll cooperate."

One-by-one, men emerged from their cover. Once they'd all joined together, Dane stepped closer. He said something out of earshot, then gestured for Eden and Jasper to follow.

"Not happening!" Jasper shouted. "This is voo-doo," he said under his breath. "How do we know all of this isn't an act? This Dane character could be one of them."

"Stop. I've known him forever—much longer than Leo. Trust me, he's one of the kindest, most gentle men I know."

"Eden! Come!" Dane urged her forward.

"How do we know we can trust you?" Jasper

shouted before she'd even opened her mouth.

"Will this help?" He pulled a menacing looking gun of the sort she'd only seen in movies out from under his coat and shot man after man in rapid-fire succession.

Eden retched.

Jasper held her.

"That's for what you did to my friends!" Dane dropped the last man standing, then crumpled to his knees. He pitched the gun a good three feet away.

"Damn . . ." Jasper slowly exhaled.

Eden escaped Jasper's hold to run to her old friend. "That was either very stupid or very brave," she said through tears. "I didn't even know you knew how to shoot."

"I don't," Dane admitted, shaky while pushing himself to his feet. "I just put my hand on the trigger and hoped for the best. I stole this gun from them on the flight over."

Still a nervous wreck herself, Eden slipped her arm around his waist for a sideways hug. "Thank you. That was horrible, but now we're all free."

"Free to do what?" Jasper asked. "The wind is picking up and it's not exactly balmy. And if the helicopter comes back, what then? Do you really trust Leo's gang to fly us to McMurdo?"

"They never had the chance to radio the pilot," Dane said. "But their snowcats are parked at the canyon entrance—the pilot picked them up there. I was already onboard. All we have to do is hike to them, and voila—we're saved."

"Interesting . . . If you're telling the truth."

"Jasper, stop. Dane is one of the good guys. He killed those men to save us."

"Whatever." He picked up their dropped gear and Dane's weapons.

This wasn't the Jasper she knew. He didn't used to be so paranoid. But then how much had she really known about him?

"Let's get going," he said. "We've got a long hike out of here and it's not getting warmer.

"Jovial fella," Dane said for only her to hear. "How did you get mixed up with him?"

"We used to date back in Denver. Remember? I was talking with him the day I dropped the sat phone . . ." Her voice trailed off when her mind's eye drifted to the horror of that day.

"What's with his attitude?"

"He's a Navy SEAL—well, used to be. Now, he does bodyguard work. I guess it's part of his job description to believe the worst of people until they prove themselves loyal."

"Makes sense. Has he taken good care of you?"

"The best. Promise, once you get to know him, you'll like him as much as I do."

"Less chitchat, more walking," Jasper said.

"When will I start liking him?" Dane asked.

Eden laughed.

Time passed almost pleasantly while hiking back to their original cat.

Upon arrival, just being out of the wind made her shoulders sag in relief. Once Jasper added heat, the vehicle's interior felt downright tropical.

The canyon was so narrow where they'd parked that he had to drive in reverse for a mile. Upon turning, they made it six miles closer to the mouth before running out of fuel.

By then, it was two a.m. and Eden could hardly keep her eyes open.

Dane had long since fallen asleep in the back.

Jasper, on the other hand, looked pensive, tapping his index fingers against the steering wheel while staring at the remaining path. She strained to hear when he whispered, "Let's ditch him."

"What? Why?"

He glanced over his shoulder. "I don't trust him."

"You should. No way am I leaving him out here to die. He doesn't even have a sleeping bag."

"We'll leave one. And food. He'll be fine until we send the authorities back from McMurdo to fetch him."

"I'm going to pretend we didn't have this conversation. Dane is a second father to me. When I lost my mother, he was a rock when my own father couldn't be. I love him."

Jasper clenched his whisker-stubbled jaw.

"Trust me." She cupped her hand to his forearm. "He's a wonderful man."

He snorted, refusing to meet her gaze.

How could they be so close on some levels, yet miles apart on others? An infinitesimal voice wondered if Jasper could be right, but then sanity stepped in. This was one more reason why they shouldn't be together. What they'd shared hadn't been real. More like a brief, intense fantasy that dulled when brought out of her bedroom and into the glaring sun.

She scowled at Jasper, then reached over the seat to jostle Dane's knee. "Wake up. Time to walk again."

He was slow to open his eyes, but then jolted upright from a slouch. "Everything all right?"

"Fine." Eden cast Jasper another dirty look before slipping on her coat. "We ran out of fuel, so we'll have to hoof it the rest of the way."

"Ugh," Dane said with a good-natured smile. "Not the best news, but even this temporary reprieve helped."

"With three of us," Jasper said, "I want to take more gear."

"Why?" Eden slipped on her hat and gloves. "We already have more than we could ever need for a fast trip to McMurdo to find help. Our station is on the way, if it looks clear, let's stop to search for my father. Leo's cats were way faster than ours. They probably have longer-range fuel tanks, as well, but just to be safe, we can refuel."

"Good call," Dane said.

"You would know this how?" Jasper asked. "Thought you never left the chopper?"

"How do you think I got to the chopper? There are plenty more cats where these came from. Did you miss the part where I told you Leo is *very* well-funded?" Dane cocked his brow. "Please don't think me overly forward, but have I done something to offend you? I don't feel comfortable with your level of animosity."

"Take it or leave it." Jasper left the cat, closing the driver's side door behind him.

"Sorry," Eden said. "I don't know what's gotten into him."

"It's okay. I'm actually glad he's on our side." He winked. "I wouldn't want him as an enemy."

The trek to Leo's cats thankfully proved uneventful, although the climb over Jasper's newly made snow and ice mountain had her sweating.

Once there, Jasper insisted on driving. Eden protested, but was too exhausted for much of a fight.

Dane didn't even try staying awake, preferring to settle onto one of the rear seats, using his heavy parka for a pillow. It made her smile when he was comfy enough to start snoring.

"Won't you at least stop long enough for a

nap?" she asked Jasper.

"Not a chance. If you want to stop off at your father's station to check if he's there and Leo's not, we'll try it. But I'm driving."

"Why do you have to be so stubborn?"

His sideways glance was still steal-her-breath gorgeous, but since adding Dane to their group, Jasper's personality had taken on a hard edge. She didn't like it. But given their circumstances, Jasper's mood swing was the least of her worries. They had to find her dad before Leo did. After that, she'd have time to mourn her lost friends while letting authorities figure out what to do with the criminal elements who had descended upon their formerly enchanted corner of the world.

As for what happened after that? Once she returned to Denver?

She hadn't thought it through. The last thing she wanted was for Jasper to bring this level of steely-eyed intensity to finding her a cure. Her mother hadn't had the blessing of dying gracefully, but Eden was determined that she would.

They'd driven for hours when the familiar sight of her father's station grew steadily larger on the horizon.

"What do you think?" Jasper braked when they were still a mile out. "See anything out of the ordinary that makes you believe Leo and his pals may be here?"

"Looks good to me." The four prefab pods looked eerily vacant. No vehicles were parked in the open-doored garages. Even the six snowmobiles were gone. "Our sat phone and internet were down when all of this started, but we could try fixing it. Leo's men destroyed the radio room, but Dad has back-ups for every system.

Far from Jasper looking encouraged by this news, he looked even deeper in thought. "Let's look for your dad. Get rest. Refuel. After that, you and I are following through with the plan to get to McMurdo."

"What about Dane?" she whispered, glancing over the seat at his sleeping form. "We're not leaving him. What if Leo's men come back?"

"Not my problem." The cat lurched forward, then settled into a smooth forward progress. Eden wished she could say the same for her and Jasper's relationship. If anything, she felt less connected. When had he grown callous enough to believe someone she trusted completely could be as guilty as Leo?

Wasn't Leo a trusted family friend? her conscience nagged. *What if Jasper is right, and Dane is no longer the man you believe him to be?*

She refused to believe Dane was anything other than the sweetheart she'd always known him to be.

They arrived at the station without further incident.

She wasn't sure what she'd expected, but normalcy wasn't it.

Warmth that was the comfort equivalent of stepping into a heated blanket.

Everything looked much as it had when they'd left. White walls and blue carpet. Rec room tables and chairs were all in place. Pinball machines beckoned with flashing lights. The pool table was set up for a game. All that was missing were the scientists, students, and support crew who made the otherwise sterile environment a home. Posters featuring sandy beaches and aqua water had poorly Photoshopped headshots of the six crew members who'd wintered-over taped to the bodies of the people lounging in the sun.

All six were now dead.

Eden looked away.

How had Leo snapped to such a degree? Had there been signs he'd been headed for a mental break?

"Home sweet home," Dane quipped, touching the photos of their fallen friends. "If you two want to look for Carl, then work on solving our communications problem, I'll cook everyone a nice, hot meal." He crossed into the small, but well-stocked industrial kitchen. "I make a mean cheeseburger and fries."

"Sounds like heaven," Eden said. "Thanks."

"You're not touching our food."

"Really?" Dane released a put-upon sigh. "Suit yourself. Eden, my love, would you like one of my world-famous burgers?"

"Only if you're adding pickles, mayo and extra cheese."

"Will do." After a quick smile, he got to work.

Jasper said under his breath, "Come with me."

"Actually . . ." Shoulders squared and chin raised, she said, "I'd rather stay with Dane. At least he's turning lemons into lemonade."

"Oh—that's rich, coming from the woman who gets one rough diagnosis, then closes up shop and settles in to die."

"Did I hear something about pie?" Dane called.

"Screw you," she said for only Jasper to hear. "You don't know a thing about me or what I've been through, so save your judgement for someone who cares."

Jasper gave her a long, hard stare, shook his head, then walked away.

She hugged herself. Why, without him, did she feel colder than if she'd still been outside in the snow? How was it that they were here together, right back where they'd started, but emotionally felt thousands of miles apart?

8

Jasper had never been much of a ladies man.

He wasn't the wine and roses type—more like the kind of guy who showed his affection through changing a girl's oil or mowing her lawn. In this instance, he would die before letting harm come to Eden. In what seemed like another lifetime, he'd placed his trust in the wrong friend, and because of that mistake, his sister-in-law had died. If protecting Eden meant coming across like a jackass, then so be it.

Something about this Dane character rubbed him the wrong way.

All three of them searched for Eden's father, but the station was deserted save for poor Doug. They'd found him dead in a lab. His neck had been broken.

Jasper carried him outside, where he covered his body in snow behind the station.

Eden and Dane said a few words about what a great guy he'd been.

All Jasper could think was that he was sorry for dragging Doug into this mess. In a roundabout way, he felt responsible for his death. The realization darkened his already sober mood.

Back inside, intent on repairing the down comms, Jasper marched halfway down the hall leading to the equipment room when he turned back to get Eden. He should never have left her alone.

Seconds later, he'd returned to the combined rec room and kitchen only to find she wasn't there.

Dane whistled while forming ground beef patties.

"Where is she?" Jasper asked.

"Oh, for heaven's sake, relax." Dane didn't look up from his work. "Eden's fine. She seemed exhausted, so I told her to take a shower and nap—not necessarily in that order."

"Why aren't you more concerned about Leo popping in?" Jasper hefted himself onto the nearest stainless steel counter. He snatched an apple from a fruit bowl and took a bite. After chewing and swallowing the less-than-ideal, mealy fruit, he noted, "It's almost like you know we're safe."

"What I know is that I'm hungry, and so is

Eden. Regardless of whether or not my former associate chooses now or later to stop by for a visit, we all need to eat—even you."

Jasper set the apple on the counter. Was he judging this guy too harshly?

"How long have you known Eden?"

"Just under a year."

"She and I first met on her fifth birthday. She was a beautiful girl with long dark hair and haunting green eyes." He lit a burner on the gas stove, set a cast iron skillet atop it, then added three hamburger patties. "Even at that age, I always thought her too serious. While I suppose most girls her age might have wanted a ballerina or fairy-themed party, she wanted a science party. Her father asked me to perform a few scientific magic tricks for her and her pint-sized guests. Of course, I agreed. We did silly things—showing off supersaturation by making ice pillars. Crushing cans with air pressure. Creating a cloud in a bottle. I'd earlier made a Rubin's tube that I set up on the lawn. After dark, the children and their parents were mesmerized by the fire dancing in time to Ace of Base."

"Thanks for the slide show, *pops*, but how does any of that prove you're not just as slimy as the nutball scum who's been trying to kill my ass ever since I set foot on this godforsaken iceberg?"

"It doesn't." Dane hummed while flipping the burgers. "Eden told me you're a former SEAL. I would imagine in that line of work, you were faced with all manner of unholy chaos on a daily basis. It must have been hard—determining the black and white of any given situation. Say you were given orders to clear a village of a suspected terrorist cell. But once you got there, you found those men were not only terrorists, but loving husbands and fathers. Sons of moms and dads who loved them every bit as much as any family would. On the one hand, those men were a danger to the very core of all Western society holds dear. On the other, they were the beating hearts at their own family core. Who were you to judge which family was more important?"

"Save the theological and ethical mind games. I get where you're coming from, but what about sacrificing one for the good of others? There's not much gray area to consider when it comes to taking out some bastard who has a hobby of strapping bombs to nursery school kids."

"Agreed. My apologies." He bowed his head. "I failed to make my point. All I'm getting at is that there are always two ways of looking at things. You and I are virtual strangers. As such, considering what you and Eden have been through, I don't blame you for your distrust. But please understand I love her as much as you."

Jasper lowered his gaze. He'd never said anything about loving her. But hell, maybe he did. Why else would he have been crazy enough to come all the way down here to save her?

His empty stomach launched a growling bitch-fest. He couldn't remember the last time he'd eaten, and the burgers smelled damned good. Did he risk them being poisoned?

He hopped down from his seat on the counter.

"Ah, there you are," Dane glanced up from flipping the burgers to smile at Eden. "That didn't take long."

"No hot water." While holding a towel to her wet hair, she winced. "I should've stayed dirty."

"I'll love you either way." Dane winked before adding cheese to the patties.

"How can I help?" Eden asked.

Jasper barely held back a snarl when she hugged the guy from behind. In most cases, Jasper liked to think he was a great judge of character, but when it came to Dane, he was having a tough time taking a read. Honestly? The man had done nothing overt to indicate he played for the other team. In fact, his show of shooting that copter team should have been convincing.

Except for the fact that it wasn't.

When the chopper pilot never heard from his team, why hadn't he returned to check on them? Or, if needed, bring more men? For that matter, it would have been just as easy to follow their trail here. Why hadn't they? What was keeping Leo away?

Or should Jasper be asking *who* was keeping him away?

While Eden chummed it up with Dane, Jasper paced.

He reached a general notice bulletin board where a note written in red Sharpie caught his eye. It had been dated today.

Marabella Station—

Douglas Anderson failed to return to McMurdo by his estimated arrival time, though his vehicle is absent from your station. Since your comms are down, we've left a sat phone. Please contact immediately to confirm station status.

—Roger Howard

Roger left his number scrawled on the legal pad on the table.

There was no phone.

Jasper looked under the table, next to it, on all nearby chairs, but sure enough—no phone.

"What'd you do with the phone, Dane?" Jasper strode back to the kitchen.

"Pardon?"

"Don't play dumb." Jasper wanted to charge him. He wanted to punch his stupid, smiley lights out. Out of respect for Eden, he didn't. But it was hardly a secret that she was pissed by his continued distrust of Daddy Dane. "See this?" He waved the note in Dane's now expressionless face. "Roger says he left a sat phone on the table. Have you seen a phone?"

"No. And I resent the fact that you're blaming me for an act I had no part in. You've been with me since we all set foot in the station. When would I have even had time to take it?"

"I'm sure there's a perfectly logical explanation." Of course, Eden jumped to Dane's defense. Maybe that was Dane's game, to turn her against the one man she could actually trust. But was that entirely true? She'd asked him to respect her wishes in the most sacred manner of allowing her to make decisions regarding her own body, and he'd not only refused, but actively plotted all the ways he'd work to find her a cure the second they returned to civilization. There was no way he'd let her die.

"Like what?" Jasper waved his hands. "Did it up and decide to spend the day hot air ballooning?"

"You're losing it." Tears shining in her eyes, Eden shook her head. "I used to think of you as my rock, but now you've become a cold, cynical man. For the last time, Dane is one of my, and my father's, dearest friends. Respect that relationship or walk to McMurdo.

Jasper balled his hands into fists.

Stepping between him and Dane, she reached out to skim both of their arms. "Nothing would make me happier than for the two of you to be friends."

"Is that your missing phone?" Dane pointed to the last row of tables. "On the floor next to that sweatshirt?"

Jasper hadn't been able to spot it from his initial point of view, but from his current angle, the phone was in plain sight.

"You owe Dane an apology," Eden said.

The hell I do. How had the phone gotten from the table to the floor? Santa and his elves hung out at the North Pole—not the south. One time too many, he'd taken a man at his word—a friend—and it had ended up bad. His sister-in-law, Mariah, hadn't just been his brother's wife, but Jasper's confidant and friend. The fact that she'd died because of his asinine stupidity had driven the entire course of his adult life. After her funeral, he'd joined the Navy because his family wanted nothing to do with him. Ever since, everything he'd ever done had been with the sole hope of making them proud. Making them love him again. His fling with Eden was never supposed to have gone further. But it had. And now, in some mixed-up, impossible to understand way, she'd become a second Mariah. A woman he loved and respected and above all, needed to protect.

Because of his blind hatred for his old pal who'd long ago duped him, could he be distrusting Dane for no better reason than a ten-year-old grudge against a guy who'd long since been locked away for dealing?

"Jasper? The burgers are ready. Come eat."

He jolted at the sudden warmth of Eden's hand on his back.

"Where were you? You seemed lost in another world."

"I was." *But I'm here now.* The past is in the past—where it needs to stay, and if any of them were going to get out of this alive, he had to set his mind to answering at least a few of the far too many questions surrounding this supposed treasure.

"Figures." She'd picked up the phone and tried calling Roger's number. "No signal." She set it on the legal pad. "We'll try again after lunch."

Lunch. What was he going to do? His every instinct screamed at him to pitch Dane's meal straight into the nearest round file, but Eden would freak. On the flip side, what if she ate it, and then dropped dead?

"O-M-G." She groaned after her first bite. "This is delicious. Thank you."

While Jasper had wasted time contemplating whether or not Dane would try poisoning them both, the woman he was supposed to be protecting could already be in grave need of medical attention.

"After we eat," Dane said, "I think we should look over your father's office. Maybe we'll find a clue to where he could be." He carried two plates from the kitchen, setting one next to her, then taking the other for himself. "Eat, Jasper. We'll need our energy for tearing this entire station apart. If you'd like, take my burger." He offered his plate.

Classic psychology. Making him believe he hadn't poisoned his own food, when in actuality, Dane planned all along for Jasper to eat his serving. Or could Dane be a step ahead of him and already suspect he'd ask to switch plates, so he hadn't?

Geez. Jasper clamped the heels of his hands to his forehead. He was starting to sound crazy even to himself. Odds were Dane was the kindly second father Eden believed him to be. If he weren't, wouldn't he be with Leo?

Jasper took the chair next to Eden and across from Dane. When the first bite of his burger didn't do him in, he took another and another, practically inhaling the whole thing.

"Hungry?" Eden asked with a sleepy-sexy grin.

He pressed the napkin Dane had also thoughtfully provided to his lips. "Thanks, man. You cook a mean burger."

"My pleasure. Glad you enjoyed it."

While Dane and Eden finished their meals, Jasper asked her, "What do you think we stand to find in your dad's office?"

"I have no idea. Dane?"

"First, I guess we need a hint as to where he could possibly be. Maybe we'll find it there, maybe not. But we have to try. We can't just leave him out there—tired and cold."

"But wait—" Eden set down her burger. "Didn't you tell me you saw Dad on a sub? If he escaped from there—I'm assuming it was somehow near shore. And did he have a boat to get to shore? Yet in all that time, Leo's goons weren't able to catch up with him?"

"Guess not." Dane kept eating. "Your dad stays fit."

"Yeah, but what did he do for foul weather gear? And what about the whiteout? If he was caught in that, then . . ."

Jasper had been proud of her for questioning Dane's explanation regarding her dad, but when he saw tears well in her eyes, he wanted to slip his arm around her shoulders, giving her a reassuring squeeze. But the timing didn't seem right. "I'm sure he's fine. Wherever he is, we'll find him."

"That's the spirit," Dane said. "My thoughts exactly. You two kids head to Carl's office. I'll clean up here."

"Are you sure?" Eden asked.

"Of course. Plus, I wouldn't mind a trip to the facilities." He winked.

"*Oooh.*" She nodded in understanding.

"Go ahead. I'll catch up."

Jasper stood, holding out his hand to Eden.

She eyed his offer of peace, then stood on her own.

They'd made it a third of the way down the hall

leading to the science lab before Jasper said, "Look, if you're pissed about the way I've been treating Dane—sorry. Some shit—stuff—went down in my past that was beyond ugly. I trusted a friend and he let me down in the worst possible way. I almost didn't earn my Trident—not because of any lack of smarts or physical endurance, but because I couldn't allow myself to trust. Once I accepted the fact that those men were my brothers, and that they'd give their very lives for me, as I would for any of them, my whole life changed."

"What happened?" She cupped her hand around his forearm. Did it make him less of a man that her simplest touch warmed him from the inside out?

"This isn't the time or place. Just know that be-cause I trusted someone I shouldn't have, my sister-in-law died."

She paled. "My God . . ."

"Since then . . ." He was beyond ashamed. "I-I not only have a tough time trusting others, but my own gut feelings. But for you, with Dane, I'm going to take your word for it that he's solid."

Wrapping her arms around him, she held him despite her anger. His own mother and father had yet to forgive him, yet here was this amazing woman who, with only the briefest explanation, was offering him comfort rather than judgement. Did he deserve it?

When she backed away, he again offered her his

hand. This time, she took it.

His soul smiled.

"My father's lab is the last door on the left. I wanted to go to his office after the attack, but there wasn't time."

They walked hand-in-hand until the narrow entry forced them apart.

She flipped a switch, drenching the dark room in light.

It was the sort of lab he'd only seen in passing when he'd been in the wrong building at the college where Eden taught. Long counters held test tubes and electronic gadgets it would take a man fifteen levels above his paygrade to understand. Shades had been lowered on two small windows. The plants on the sills had died.

"His personal office is through here." She led Jasper through a windowless storage area and into a dark square room. In a land of eternal sun, his eyes revolted to adjusting to the dark.

After a fumble for the wall switch, he was blinking again from the sudden change. And then he was holding Eden when she gasped, and then burst into tears.

The office hadn't merely been ransacked, but destroyed.

"Will this ever end?" Falling to her knees, she gathered framed photos of her and a beautiful, smiling dark-haired woman Jasper assumed was her mother. The glass was broken, so he joined her in removing the precious photos from their ruined frames.

"I'm sorry, babe. We'll get new frames once we hit civilization."

"It's not just the frames," she said with a sniffle, drying her eyes with her T-shirt's long sleeves. "My father gave his entire life to this place. To finding a cure for the disease that ravaged my mother and will soon have its grips solidly on me. He gave his whole life to save us, only to have it all reduced to this silly, stupid quest for a treasure that doesn't even exist."

"We'll clean it up, okay? We'll clean it and find some clue as to why all of this is even happening. We'll find your dad. And then together—you, me and Dane—we'll rescue him, and then we'll all go home."

"I don't even have a place to stay in Denver. I sold it. *Everything*. I was never going back. There was no point."

"All of that's changed." On his knees, he cupped her dear face in his hands, drawing her close for a kiss he prayed held a fraction of the love he felt for her at that moment. "When this is over—whatever it turns out to be—you're mine. I won't let you go."

"Jasper . . . You have to get it through your thick, handsome head that even you can't save me."

Ignoring her belief, choosing to know that to-gether they'd beat any obstacles in their way, he eased his lips into a slow grin. "You think I'm handsome?"

At the door, Dane cleared his throat. "Is this a private party?"

Eden lurched back as if her own father had caught her making out. "Dane. You startled me."

"My apologies. I'm here to help." He shook his head and sighed. "Judging by this mess, you two could use an extra pair of hands."

"I don't even know where to start, least of all what we're looking for. And besides, wouldn't we be better off searching the area where Dad ran from the sub? There's no shelter for hundreds of miles. He's out there somewhere—starving and cold."

Dane cupped his hand to her shoulder. "You and I both know your father's a fighter. No matter what, he'll stay alive."

"I'm with Dane on this, babe. I only met your dad once back in Denver, but he seemed like the sort of Indiana Jones-type who could handle pretty much anything and win."

"Except snakes," Dane added with a smile. "Like the movie character, Carl always did hate snakes—maybe that's why he has such an affinity for being on the ice."

"I take it he liked rocks, too?" Jasper shuffled through the debris to pick up a baseball-sized chunk.

"That's a meteorite," Eden noted. "He has dozens. It's a hobby—at least, it used to be. When my mom was alive, we used to take weekend trips to a valley fairly close to here that was strewn with them. While they looked for those beauties, I played house in a little cave. Mom even helped me make curtains out of an old sheet." Wearing a wistful smile, she sat back on her heels.

"A cave, you say?" Dane set the papers he'd gathered on the desk. "How far back did it go? Could your father be there now for shelter?"

"It's at least an eight-hour trek from here—and that was in a cat. It would take days on foot."

"Look what I found." Jasper handed Eden a faded receipt for an item he knew she held dear. "This looks so old your dad probably forgot he even had it."

Her eyes teared upon reading the fragile document. "I had no idea it cost so much . . ."

"What is it?" Dane asked.

"The receipt for my locket." Eden fingered the gold heart. "He paid over ten grand. The amethyst's tiny. Hate to say it, but Dad got rooked."

"It is beautiful," Jasper offered.

"That does seem high." Dane's eyebrows furrowed. "I remember when your father ordered it. He was excited for you to have a special gift for your twelfth birthday. May I see it?"

"My locket? Sure." She fumbled for the clasp, but had trouble reaching it beneath her long ponytail.

"I'll help," Dane stood behind her. While she lifted her hair, he undid the clasp. "I haven't seen it since the day he wrapped it. Wonder how the receipt came to be in his office down here?"

"Look at all this stuff. Dad always was a pack rat. It probably got mixed in with something he'd printed. He never was a fan of web documents. If he couldn't hold it in his hand, it didn't exist."

"This is quite a chunk of gold." Dane palmed it to judge the weight. "Mind if I open it?"

"Of course not. You're probably familiar with the photo inside. It's a copy I had made of a photo snapped of the three of us when we went to Maui for Christmas. I think that was the only time we didn't spend the holidays down here—and that was only because Mom's doctor wouldn't let her travel for longer than a week."

"Impeccable workmanship." Dane closed the piece to turn it over, studying the family tree etched on the back. "I suppose this sort of artistry is expensive."

Was it Jasper's imagination, or was Dane studying the locket too closely?

"May I please have it back? I feel antsy without it."

"I don't blame you. I'll put it on." Behind her, he looped the sturdy chain around her neck to fasten.

"Thanks." She clasped the heart that symbolically held her family. "One nice thing about it being gold is that I never have to take it off. The seal is even watertight."

"Ingenious." Dane cleared his throat. "So . . . Jasper, you'll no doubt think the worst of me for this—and you'd certainly be within your rights to do so, but please know I only had our Eden's best interests at heart."

"Do I need a gun?" Jasper asked.

Eden slowly rose to her feet. "Dane? What are you talking about? We trusted you . . ."

He waved off their concerns. "I promise you're both perfectly safe in my presence. But I'm afraid I might have told a wee white lie about Carl."

"Is he hurt?" Eden paled. "Or worse?"

"No, no. Nothing like that." He was again clearing his throat as if he'd swallowed a gnat. "I, ah, am afraid I haven't seen your father since the day Leo and his men stormed the station."

"But you said—" Angry heat flamed Eden's cheeks.

How could he have lied about something so important?

"I knew you couldn't be trusted," Jasper muttered.

"Sorry. I thought it might help ease poor Eden's mind. At the time, our situation seemed fairly dire, so I didn't see the harm in sugar coating an issue so out of her control."

"Dane . . ." She sighed. "I had a right to know. So basically, my father could be back in Tampa for all we know?"

"Theoretically, I suppose. But let's look at this from a logical perspective. If folks from McMurdo sent people here to check on their missing man, it stands to reason that they would have also sent word that your father had shown up there to ask for help. You're his world, Eden. There's nothing that matters more to him than keeping you safe."

"If that's true, then why did he leave me? He asked me to go with him—to wherever he is—but I couldn't just leave my friends. By the time I caught my breath enough to find him, he was gone. What could have possibly mattered more to him than the life of his daughter and all of the people we live and work with? It doesn't make sense." She pressed her fingers to her temples. "None of this even seems real."

Jasper wrapped his arms around her, hoping his hold conveyed what he lacked the wherewithal to say. In that moment, he ached for her. Her father was her world. For him to abandon her at a time when she'd been in mortal danger was the worst kind of betrayal. Totally on par with what his old druggie friend had done to him. As much as Jasper enjoyed sharing common ground with Eden, he yearned for something better than the dark connection.

"What makes you think Carl would have gone to this cave as opposed to McMurdo? Seems illogical," Jasper asked Dane.

"Not if what Leo believes about the treasure could be true."

"Geez . . ." Jasper shook his head. "I'm still struggling with wrapping my head around this whole treasure theory."

"I was too," Dane said. "But just now when we started putting the pieces together, I can't help but wonder if Carl truly does have a treasure? One so valuable he'd guard it with his life?"

"Then he can choke on it." Eden crossed her arms.

"You don't mean that," Dane said.

"Yes, I actually do. Nothing is worth more than life—love. *Nothing.*"

Amen. Jasper's heart went out to her.

"Granted," Dane said. "But for all we know, Leo himself, or even some of his men, may have forced him there. As well as I know Carl, he must have had a compelling reason to leave you. One more thing—shortly after your mother died, your father declared bankruptcy. Her medical bills were astronomical. He felt buried under the financial pressure. Yet two years later, he paid a small fortune to buy your locket and tripled the size of this station? Does that sound like the actions of a poor man to you?"

Eden again clasped her golden heart.

"What do you want to do?" he asked her. "The snowcat is already filled with emergency supplies, plus we have McMurdo's sat phone. As long as you can lead us to where you think your old cave may be, we can go have a look, calling for backup along the way. If we find your dad, great. If we don't, at least we'll know where he isn't. Sound like a plan?"

A thump sounded from a few rooms away. Followed by a metallic bang.

"What was that?" Eyes wide, Dane stepped behind the door.

"Wait here with Eden," Jasper said. "I'll check it out."

9

"I'm sorry," dane said once Jasper left to inspect the hall. He reached out to hug Eden, but she stepped away.

"Don't touch me. I don't understand how you could be so cruel. I believed you when you said my father was safe—at least he might have had a better chance with the elements than with a killer. Now, he could be anywhere." She poked her head out from behind the door. "Jasper? Everything okay?"

When he didn't answer, her heart pounded. If something happened to him, she wasn't sure what she'd do.

She crept out to the lab.

"*Eden!*" Dane whispered. "Get back here."

"No. I'm not leaving Jasper to fend for himself."

"Are you implying that's what I did with your dad? If so, it's not true. You know what it was like when Leo and his men were here. Utter and complete chaos. It's a miracle any of us are alive."

"I know. Now, hush. With you yammering, I can't hear a thing." She crept closer and closer to the hall door but didn't hear a sound. "Jasper?"

"Look what I found." Jasper appeared. He held something, but from where he stood in the hall's shadows, she couldn't tell exactly what.

When it moved in his arms, she leaped backwards, clutching her hand to her chest. "Hope you know CPR. I need it."

"Sorry. Check him out. I didn't know pets were allowed?"

"They're not. *At all.*" Yet he held a gorgeous white Persian with ice blue eyes. She stepped closer, holding the tag on his collar. "According to this, his name is Yeti."

"Who does he belong to? And how in the world did his owner keep him a secret? I can't even begin to imagine how they smuggled him in. On a supply ship?" She took the purring cat for a cuddle. "Poor, baby. You must be starving."

"I caught him jumping from table to table in the lab across the hall. He must have knocked over a stool."

"Who in their right mind would smuggle a cat down here?" Dane emerged from the office.

"No clue," Eden said. "But now that we found him, we need to feed him, then track down what he was using for food and a litter box." To the cat she said, "Your mommy or daddy must be seriously creative." Too late she remembered whoever the cat belonged to was dead. Tears stung her eyes, and in the moment, she felt inordinately grateful for the small luxury of cuddling the giant fluffball. "I'll take care of you, okay?"

For how long she couldn't promise, but maybe Jasper would care of him once she was gone.

The thought was macabre, but Eden had watched her mother gift her most loved possessions to her most cherished friends. Because Carl was always traveling, her college roomie took Coconut the Pomeranian. When her mom died, Eden split her time between boarding schools and her father's Antarctic station. She'd never had a pet again.

Was it selfish of her to take on one now? Yes. But it wasn't as if fate had given her a choice. In this moment, maybe she needed the cat as much as he needed her.

In the dormitory pod, they all fanned out to locate the cat's hidden home.

"Found it!" Jasper called ten minutes into their search.

Eden met him toward the end of the second floor hall.

"Looks like he scratched his way out of the

room. Good thing these prefab walls are thin." A ragged hole had been clawed near the door. Piles of single-serve tuna packets were mounded in a suitcase. An empty plate and water bowl sat alongside it. A makeshift litter box had been made of a cardboard box, lined with a recycling bag, then filled with dirt. The smell wasn't exactly pleasant. "If you want to feed him and get him water, then get his food suitcase ready to go, I'll get rid of this mess, then rig up a portable box for him to use once we're on our way to the cave."

"Thank you." She stood on her tiptoes, crushing the cat between them while stealing a kiss.

The cat meowed.

"You're welcome," Jasper said. "But I think someone would rather eat than cuddle. Clearly, I'm going to have to find him a good woman when we get back to town." His wink produced a flutter low in Eden's tummy. Just when she thought she could manage fine without him, he went and showed his sweeter side—that side of him, she'd never been able to resist.

"So this is where you two scurried off to." Holding his shirt collar over his nose, Dane waved his free hand in front of his face. "Smells like it's for good reason pets aren't allowed. We're leaving him here, right?"

"He can't help his circumstance. And no, we're taking him. What if the heat goes down? Or he runs out of food or water? Or, God forbid, we run into Leo and never have the chance to send help. We'd be horrible people to leave him."

"Maybe so, but our primary focus should be rescuing your dad—not a contraband cat."

Eden ignored his harsh words in favor of feeding the starving creature.

By the time Yeti had eaten his fill, Eden had his food supply zipped and ready to go. She scooped up the cat and then wheeled the bag out into the hall filled with the ghosts of her lost friends.

Everywhere she looked were signs of the horror.

Blood splattered on a wall. A lone shoe, sweater or book.

The knot lurking at the back of Eden's throat made it tough to breathe. But for her father, for Jasper and Dane and now, even this cat, she had to keep her head clear and resolve strong.

Thirty minutes later, all new supplies had been loaded into their ride—including the cat. Jasper topped off the fuel, and Eden refreshed her memory on the meteor valley's location with the help of laminated topo maps.

Jasper had added six more cases of canned goods and spare propane canisters for the stove. He'd even found backpacks in the rec hall storage closet that would be ideal for hauling supplies, should they have to go far on foot. He'd also insisted on two complete changes of clothing for her and Dane. For his own needs, he raided a dorm room closet.

As worried as Eden was about the fate of her father, she was also that encouraged about this lead. Why hadn't she thought of it sooner?

"That's the last of it." Jasper closed the vehicle's rear cargo door. "Ready to roll?"

"Only if you'll let me drive," she said. "I can't remember the last time you slept."

"Me, neither, but it doesn't matter. Let's get going. We'll sort out who drives along the way."

"I'll drive," Dane said. "It's only fair. I had plenty of sleep on the way here."

"That's a great idea." Eden hopped in back with her fluffy friend. "Jasper, you can ride shotgun."

He shot her a death-ray stare.

"Please." She blew him a kiss. "I'm worried about you. Please, get some rest."

"I concur." Dane climbed behind the wheel. "It may have been a while since I've been at the helm of one of these cantankerous things, but I'm sure it's like riding a bike."

Jasper asked, "When's the last time you rode one of those?"

"Give or take a few dozen years." Dane winked, then laughed. "Relax, would you? Promise, if we stumble across anything of note, I'll wake you. Eden can stay awake to keep me company."

"If that's the case," she said, "how about Yeti and I ride in front? That way, Jasper can stretch out."

He reluctantly agreed, and then they were finally off.

Before falling asleep, Jasper had programmed the GPS with the valley's coordinates. Eden worried her memory might be off. After all, she hadn't been to the place in years, but she knew from a few familiar landmarks that she had to at least be in the right vicinity on the map.

Once Jasper had fallen into a deep sleep, Dane said. "He's good for you. I see why your dad likes him."

"He does?" They'd only met that one time at a Denver steakhouse while her father had been at her college for a fundraising campaign.

"Oh, yes. He's spoken of him many times, wondering if you two were anywhere near wedding bells."

Her cheeks warmed. Once upon a time, thoughts of those happy bells consumed her. Now? Considering her diagnosis, there wasn't much point. "We're both fine maintaining status quo."

"Young people today . . ."

"You never married," she jabbed.

"Ah, but I never had a woman as obviously smitten with me as our young Jasper is with you." He patted her knee, then focused on driving.

The day was one of those rare arctic gems when

the sky was so blue and clear it seemed close enough to touch. The temp hovered near the teens, making it practically beach weather. According to her re-membrances of the long ago trips she and her parents had taken, they drove due north from the station, then rode up and down over a series of small foothills before settling onto a higher, windswept plain. Much of the snow had been blown away, leaving the rough volcanic soil exposed.

The drive continued as pleasantly as if time had returned her childhood.

She and Dane shared happy memories.

Once Jasper woke, he entertained them with harrowing stories about his days as a SEAL.

Through it all, Yeti purred on her lap.

By the time they stopped for lunch, Eden was more than ready to stretch her legs. Clouds had rolled in, and the temperature had dropped back to its normally frigid negative digits.

Jasper set up the camp stove for her, and she used boiled water to prepare their freeze-dried meals.

"Dane," Eden said after her first bite. "Your hamburger beat the crap out of this beef stroganoff."

He chuckled. "I'm not too thrilled with my mac and cheese, either."

"I don't know what you guys are talking about." Jasper had already finished his teriyaki chicken, and held the bag to his mouth to get the very last drop of sauce. "Compared to some of the crap I've eaten, that was five-star dining."

Eden and Dane shared a laugh.

Yeti gave two paws way up for his tuna.

With lunch a memory, Eden behind the wheel, and Jasper holding the cat beside her, miles rolled by. The scenery changed from a stark, arid plain to an ice field strewn with eerie creature-like formations. Snow began to fall and Eden struggled to tell the difference between the sky and the horizon.

"Want me to take over?" Jasper asked.

"Thanks, but not quite yet. What time is it?"

"Eight. Past time for you to get some shut-eye."

She yawned at the mere suggestion. "You're probably right."

The whole time they'd traveled, she wondered if somehow Leo and his men were watching. If there was treasure at this cave—a ridiculous notion, but for her father's sake, one she was willing to enter-tain—was she now leading them to it? She didn't re-call the hollow even going further back than maybe ten feet.

"Babe, slow down." Jasper pointed ahead. "What's that?"

She braked.

A deep cut in the ice loomed maybe fifty yards in front of their vehicle. It was at least five feet wide and stretched as far in each direction as blowing snow allowed them to see.

Her stomach twisted. "What should we do?"

He raked his fingers through his hair. "I honestly don't have a clue."

Dane snored in back.

"Let's gear up," Jasper said. "We'll walk it a ways to see if it narrows or we can find a snow bridge."

Five minutes later, feeling like the abominable snowman in her heavy winter gear, she walked next to Jasper, squinting from the assault of icy snow. Each flake stung her exposed cheeks like pointy tacks.

"Even if we find a snow bridge, how do we know it would hold the cat's weight?"

"We don't. Which is why I'd be doing the driving."

"Are you insane? If anyone should risk his or her life, it's me."

Ignoring her comment, he walked thirty feet ahead. "It's narrow enough here for me to jump. There's rope in the cat. Once across, I could tie it off and throw it to you. If you miss the jump, I'll pull you up."

"No. And what about Dane? And Yeti?"

She'd caught up to Jasper. Judging by the stern set of his jaw, he wasn't feeling warm and fuzzy for their new pet or her father's friend. "How far is it to the cave?"

"We have to be close. But this snow is making it

impossible to judge landmarks. I remember crossing this ice field with Mom and Dad, but back then, there'd been no hazards."

"God bless global warming . . ." He shook his head.

"Yeah . . ." She couldn't believe their lousy luck.

"Can you think of any other possible way around?"

"I guess we could try, but the terrain would be too steep or uneven for our ride."

Jasper shivered. "It's cold as balls out here. When this is behind us, we're going straight to the Bahamas."

Forcing a smile, she nodded.

It would be just as easy to die there as in Denver.

She refused to give the dark thought light. With treatment, her mother lived a couple years beyond her diagnosis. Without treatment? Eden hadn't stuck around her oncologist's office long enough to find out. Her body was her greatest enemy. A ticking time bomb designed to annihilate her every hope for happiness.

"Let's get back." He grabbed her elbow, guiding her through the heavier snow and wind. "We'll look at the topo maps and decide."

An hour later, nearing whiteout conditions, they were no closer to reaching a decision.

All three of them huddled in back, pouring over

the maps with steaming mugs of hot chocolate. The GPS and sat phone were both offline.

Yeti sat on the bench seat back, reigning over the proceedings while giving himself a tongue bath.

"The way I see it," Dane pointed to the meteor-strewn valley where she'd first seen the cave. "The only option we have for avoiding the crevasse is to backtrack eighty miles to this area." He traced his finger along his proposed route. "From there, if we turn due east, we should be able hug the edge of this mountain, then find Eden's cave from the backside."

"That's a very big *if.*" Eden finished her cocoa. "Look at the terrain levels. What if we get over there to find it impassable?"

"It's a chance we'll have to take."

"Or," Jasper said. "We pack a minimum amount of gear to get us through, say, forty-eight hours. We jump the crevasse, then hike the rest of the way."

"What about Yeti?" Eden asked. "We can't leave him."

"Sweetheart . . ." Dane shot the feline a not-so-kind look. "Your father's life is at stake. Leave the creature here. If he makes it—great. If he freezes . . ."

"Are you listening to yourself?" Since when had her kindly almost-uncle adopted this selfish streak? "Absolutely not. If we're doing this, I'll carry him with me inside my parka. He'll be like my own personal heating pad."

It was midnight. Because of the storm, the sunlight had faded to gray. Wind howled with enough force to rock the vehicle with each gust.

"Should we rest up until this weather clears?" Jasper asked.

"No." Dane smacked the heel of his hand against the nearest window. "If Carl is in that cave. We must reach him. Time is of the essence."

"So is our strength," Jasper reasoned. "Visibility's about two-feet. If we can barely see our hands in front of our faces, how the hell are we supposed to find a cave Eden hasn't been to since she was a little girl?"

Dane bowed his head. "I see your point."

"We're in agreement?" he looked from Eden to Dane. "We'll start hiking as soon as the weather clears?"

"Agreed," Eden said.

Dane nodded, but didn't meet either of their stares.

Though exhausted, Eden struggled to sleep.

She and Jasper bedded down in the cargo area. Dane took the backseat.

Hours later, the wind turned violent, scaring Yeti to the point that he squirmed into Eden's bag.

"Are you awake?" she whispered to Jasper.

"Sort of. My brain's too cold to sleep."

She rolled over to face him. Yeti repositioned to curl against her tummy. "Do you think my dad could really be all the way out here?"

"Tough to say. It is feasible—especially if he took one of the snowmobiles. But you think the cave doesn't go much further back than ten feet?"

"Not the way I remember. But who knows?"

"Not to change the subject . . ." He wormed and wriggled his bag closer to hers. "But I heard we could generate major body heat if we zipped our bags together and got naked." His toothy grin shone in the unnerving gloom.

"Mmm . . ." The thought of pressing herself to him, skin-to-skin, instantly had her humming between her legs. "Tempting offer. But in order to get to you, I'd have to leave my cozy nest. Plus, Yeti would be pissed."

"Damned cat." He leaned closer for a kiss.

With them both wrapped like mummies, the simple brush of his lips to hers by most would have been considered chaste, but the fog of his warm, familiar breath on her upper lip made her feel as if she were falling into a bed of cotton candy. Soft and dizzyingly sweet.

"I really do want to go to the Bahamas with you," she whispered after he deepened their latest kiss, thrilling her with the sweep of his tongue.

"Then we'll make it happen."

"Promise?" Her pulse quickened while awaiting his response.

"Absolutely." He kissed her lips once more, then the tip of her nose. "Now, go to sleep."

With him holding her hand, she finally did.

Eden woke to bright sun.

The wind had died, and Jasper was already at work, making oatmeal and coffee.

Yeti hunkered over a tuna-filled metal bowl.

"Thanks for feeding him," she said.

"You're welcome. Good morning—only it's three in the afternoon."

She groaned. "Where's Dane?"

"Checking out the crevasse. While you slept, we walked further down and found a sweet snow bridge that's about ten feet wide. It seems sturdy enough to walk across, but we've reinforced it by making a bridge of sorts out of the supply tub lids." He handed her a steaming foil oatmeal packet.

"Thanks. So how did you make a bridge out of lids?"

"We melted about eight holes at each end, then wove rope through to lace them together. Once we had four connected, we put two holes in the end of each of those, then roped them to tent stakes. I anchored them good on either side, so even if the snow gives out beneath us, our bridge should hold long enough to get us safely across."

"I hate that you risked your life by crossing before you even knew it was safe."

"Couldn't be helped."

Yes, it could have. If they abandoned this search that more than likely would end in failure. "I probably don't want to know the answer, but when we're done at the cave, if the bridge does break, how do we get back?"

"How about we cross that bridge when we get to it? *Da da dum*." He performed a playful drumbeat on the side of the metal stove. "Even under pressure, I've got superstar appeal."

"You're a mess." She dug into her hearty meal.

"But you love me."

Yes. More and more she did. But was that a good thing?

Dane returned to eat.

By the time they'd all finished, then packed enough gear and food to cover most any contingency, they set out into brilliant sunlight. The glare was so bright that Eden winced even behind dark, tinted glasses. Cold air seared her lungs.

They reached the bridge ten minutes later.

Just looking at the thing made Eden's oatmeal ride back up.

The bottom of the crevasse was fathomless. A fall would mean not only instant death, but that her body wouldn't be found until the next greenhouse era. She liked to think she had this cancer thing under control—that she was at peace with it being close to her time to go. But in that moment, nothing could be further from the truth.

Her palms were sweating inside of her gloves and the more Yeti fidgeted in the bib of her overall-style snow pants, the more panicked she grew.

Dane had already crossed, and now Jasper made his third trek over with supplies.

He made it look easy, so why did Eden's limbs feel leaden with dread?

Finished with the gear, Jasper crossed to her side, holding out his hands. "Hand me Yeti. I don't want him panicking on you midway through your trip."

"I'm not sure I can do this." She held out the cat.

Yeti hissed at the cold, and was all too happy when Jasper settled him beneath his coat.

"Of course you can." Jasper led her to the edge. "One foot at a time. No big deal. It's surprisingly sturdy."

"You can do it," Dane coached from the other side. "Just don't look down."

As if on cue, a frosty updraft chafed her cheeks. Never had Jasper's proposed trip to the Bahamas sounded better.

Knowing if they were to stand a chance at finding the cave where her father might be hiding, she had to go across. She was the only one who could lead them to its exact location. She forced a deep breath. Sharp wind brought tears to her eyes.

"You've got this, babe."

Eden's heart thundered loud enough to hear it in her ears. She took one step onto the hard plastic lids, then another. Midway through, she made the mistake of looking down at the icy blue. A wave of vertigo swirled her off balance, but she fought her way through. By the time she reached Dane, he had to hold her upright, because her legs were too rubbery to stand.

"Great job!" Jasper shouted from where she'd come. "I see rappelling in our futures."

"No way!" She laughed in relief.

"We'll start off at a nice, safe indoor climbing gym." He removed his gloves. Shoved them in his pockets so he could give her pet a rub. Had there ever been a sweeter man?

He stepped onto the bridge. One more step took him to the middle.

Yeti poked his head out of Jasper's partially unzipped jacket, caught sight of his surroundings and bolted.

Jasper lunged for the cat, but missed. In the process, throwing himself off balance, and falling.

Eden screamed.

10

Jasper drew his upper lip into his mouth and clamped down. Hard.

With his legs swinging, his arms screamed from the effort of holding his bodyweight with only the thin plastic lid for support.

He glanced up to see the damned cat leap safely across, but he wasn't sure how to rescue himself.

"Hold on." Dane tossed a rope onto the bridge. "Let me tie this off to a rock, and I'll help drag you up."

Now was hardly the time to admit he still didn't fully trust Dane. But he didn't. He had one shot to grab the rope. If he missed, he died. If Dane had failed to tie-off the rope properly, he died. If he tried hauling himself over the snow bridge's side and his weight caused it to collapse . . .

Yeah, pretty much in every scenario he bit the big one.

"Okay! The rope's tied off." Dane ran to the chasm's edge. "Grab for it, Jasper! I've got you!"

Trust was a funny thing. With his life literally hanging in the balance, the irony wasn't lost on him that never more than in this moment had he been forced to follow his own gut instinct.

"Please, Jasper! Grab the rope!" Eden's voice rose above his mind's chaos. Even above his heart's rhythmic roar.

His mouth had gone dry.

His fingertips had long-since turned numb.

"Jasper! The rope!" Trust. It all came down to this moment. Eden's voice spurred him on. He'd learned to trust again with his SEAL brothers, and now was the time to forever imprint the lesson in his heart with her and Dane. Most importantly—*himself.*

"*Jasper!*"

He forced what could be his last breath, then leapt.

His palms slapped against the nylon rope, and though he could no longer feel his fingers, they miraculously still managed to grab. He had taken a firm hold of the rope, but still fell deeper and terrifyingly deeper, certain he'd made the worst mistake in his life by believing in Dane. But then with a sharp twang, the rope stopped his fall.

He crashed face-first into the ice wall. Tasted blood on his tongue.

But the rope held and Dane was pulling him up.

A few feet from the top, Jasper reached for the crevasse's edge, and pulled himself the rest of the way to safety.

"*Ohmygod . . .*" Eden knelt beside him, cupping her hand to his forehead and cheeks. "Are you okay? Does anything hurt?"

The damned cat had the audacity to brush against Jasper's face.

"Bit my tongue. I'm sure I'll have a few bruises, but other than that, I'm fine. Dane? Where are you?"

"Right here." He slowly approached, then bent at the waist, bracing his hands against his knees. "You gave me quite a workout. I vote that jinx cat off the island."

"It was an accident." Jasper groaned while pushing himself upright. "Could have happened to anyone, but I'm glad it was me. Poor guy would have starved had something happened to his *mother.*" He winked.

"How can you crack a joke at a time like this?" Tears froze at the corners of her eyes. "You could have died. I'm worried sick about my dad, but the odds of him being all the way out here seem infinitesimal. We have no business being out here and should turn back. Head straight for McMurdo."

"We will," Dane said. "But we've already come

this far. Why not at least check the cave? That way, we'll have a definitive answer one way or the other. We'll be that much closer to finding Carl."

Eden's conscience forced her to agree.

For the next six hours, they trudged over the ice field to finally arrive in the meteor-strewn valley where she'd played as a child.

With her eyes closed, she saw her mom and dad, strolling hand-in-hand on the warmest of summer days. She saw herself setting up her dolls in the shallow cave. As a special treat, they'd once even spent the night in the shelter.

At the base of the trail they'd climb to reach it, Eden's mother had built a rock cairn, then taught her how to construct her own. Would they still be there?

Her pulse picked up as she pushed herself to quicken her pace. She really hoped they'd be there. She needed them to be, to serve as a reminder that this small part of her mother's legacy endured.

After another hour, they rounded a bend, and there they were—as solid as the day she and her mom had made them. Only now, there were three. Had her father made one, too? Could Dane be right and he was here?

She ran.

"Dad!" Cold air seared her lungs like icy fire, but she kept on charging up the hill. "Dad, are you here? We've come to help!"

Until this moment, she hadn't realized how terrified she'd been of losing him. After all she'd already been through, having her father die was unthinkable. But as she gritted her teeth through the most grueling portion of the trail, she got her first look in the cave to see it was deserted.

Hope deflated, rushing from her chest as if her soul had sprung a leak.

She sat on a rock, covering her face with gloved hands. Her eyes stung, but it was too cold to even cry.

"Sorry, babe." Jasper slipped his arm around her shoulders. "At least we tried. Even though he's not here, we'll find him, okay?"

She nodded. He was sweet to comfort her, but this was an ache too deep to touch.

"I was so sure . . ." Dane ducked to enter the shallow passage.

From this vantage, gray sky blended with rock, making the inhospitable landscape all the more foreign. She didn't belong here. Her parents' vibrancy and love was what made this place special. Without them, it was just another forbidding mountain that wanted them gone.

Yeti squirmed against her chest.

She helped him out, setting him to the frost-covered ground. He darted for the cavern, so she followed. If he did his business in there, she'd need to collect it. Out of respect for her dad, she'd do her best to maintain biological protocol.

"Let me get him." Jasper brushed past.

The tight place smelled of dust. A trace of sulphur from a nearby volcanic vent.

"He's gone," Jasper stood at the cave's narrow end.

"Good riddance," Dane said. "Let's get back to our rolling heater."

Ignoring Dane's snide remark, Eden asked Jasper, "What do mean he's *gone*? There's nowhere to go." This far back, light was nonexistent. The vacuum of black made her beyond uneasy.

"Do me a favor," Jasper knelt at the back wall, "and get a flashlight from my pack. Should be in one of the zippered side pockets."

She returned a minute later to hand him the tool. He flicked it on, running it along the wall's base until spotting a softball-sized hole. He placed his hand in front of it. "Feel that?"

Kneeling beside him, she removed her bulky glove to place her palm near the hole. A gush of warmer air blew against her skin.

"What's taking so long?" Dane complained. "I thought we were leaving?"

"Hold up." Jasper slipped his fingers between what they could now see wasn't the cave wall, but a rock pile. "We might have found something."

"Unless it's a steaming plate of lasagna, I'm not interested."

"Hold this." Jasper handed her the light, then

began the arduous task of shifting large stones.

Meow. Yeti poked his head from the hole.

"Oh, for heaven's sake," Dane joined them. "We should—*oh my*. Does the cave go further back after all?"

"Looks like it," Jasper said. "Give me a hand moving these rocks."

Yeti performed figure-eights around Eden's ankles.

Finished, the men stood back to appraise a two foot-by-three foot passage.

"Carl?" Dane shouted into the black.

Eden held her breath while waiting for a response.

"Eden, do you remember this rock pile being here from when you were a kid?" Jasper asked.

"I don't know. I mean, I guess it could have been. I never came this far back. It was too dark."

Jasper took the light from her, then duck-walked deeper into the passage. "Holy shit . . ."

"Is there treasure?" Dane asked.

"Better." Poking his head out of the hole, Jasper's whisker-stubbled face was dirt smudged, but still gorgeous. "Footprints. Let's put on headlamps and see where they go."

"Wait—" Eden shook her head, trying not to get too excited. "Are they fresh? I mean, can you even tell that sort of thing?"

"Yes and yes. Which means your dad—or

someone else who was recently here, went to a lot of trouble to hide their tracks going in. Now, the only question is—was that person your father, or one of Leo's gun-toting thugs?"

11

"Is anyone else thinking this tunnel is too pre-cise to be natural?" Jasper had been leading Eden, Dane and Yeti deeper into the cavern for for-ty-five minutes and had yet to come to a fork in their gravel-floored road.

"Yes," Dane said, "but how can that be? To cre-ate something of this scale would take tremendous resources—not to mention time."

"Dane, if you're back to thinking we'll find a pot of gold at the end of this rainbow, you're wrong. You know how absorbed Dad is in his studies. He might have long ago found this place, and sealed it for safety, but I'm guessing we're walking through an ancient lava tube."

The rush of running water echoed through the

foreboding space.

The only other sounds were the crunch of their boots on lifeless dirt.

On and on they walked until the trail reached a dead-end at a black underground river. Their head-lamps sparked on the view, making the water look as if it were undulating and alive.

"How do we get across?" Dane asked.

"We don't . . . Check it out." He aimed his light at a squared alcove that had been chiseled into the stone. Lined in a row were three gray inflatables, covered in dust. There was space available for many more. Twenty dusty canvas life preservers from a bygone era hung on a rack beside them, along with a metal box with the words: *Erste Hilfe*.

"My God . . ." Dane took a step back. "It's true."

"What are we looking at?" Eden asked. "What does that say?"

"It's a first aid kit—my guess, Nazi."

"No way . . ." She lifted Yeti into the safety of her arms.

"For years," Dane danced his hands along the white metal case as if it were covered in diamonds, "there have been stories about a hidden Antarctic Nazi base, but I never believed them. There were reportedly covert German military operations in a vast underground complex in Queen Maud Land. But this is nowhere near that. Hitler was supposedly fanatical about having more than one point of entry and egress from any compound. This tunnel could be one. The river could lead to the actual facility. We must go. *Immediately*. Jasper, help." He tugged on the line holding the remaining rafts in place.

"Look," Jasper said, "I love a conspiracy theory as much as the next guy, but mostly on a Saturday night after downing a couple six-packs. This is . . ." He swept his arms open wide, shaking his head. "This is fucking nuts—pardon my French. There's no way I'm letting Eden climb into one of those ancient rafts. The rubber's got to be brittle as hell. If we fall into that water—well, it's suicide. Not happening."

"Yes, it is." Her voice barely rose above the water's roar. "If my father is down here, I have to know."

"That's the spirit," Dane said. "Onward!"

"Eden . . ." Jasper went to her, planting his hands on her shoulders. "Listen to what you're saying. That river could lead anywhere. For all we know, it leads straight to nowhere. I don't know about you, but drowning in a cold-ass, black whirlpool doesn't top my list of preferred ways to go."

They locked stares in the gloom.

He knew what she was thinking. That even if they lived beyond this moment, the cancer would soon claim her.

She defiantly raised her chin.

"Eden, please . . ." He'd long since removed his gloves, and now skimmed his palms over her hair. "You don't want to do this."

"It's not a matter of *wanting* to," she said. "I have to. What if it was your father who was lost? Wouldn't you do anything to find him?"

What a loaded question. Considering no one in his family had talked to him for years, he had no way to answer. Of course, he would love reuniting with his relatives, but at this moment, Eden and Dane and even the stupid cat felt more closely related. Sure, he had his SEAL brothers whom he knew he could always count on, but on a deeper level, this was as much of a family as he'd been part of since Mariah died.

"A little help?" Dane tugged hard enough on the raft stays that the entire pile toppled. A dust cloud rose. He erupted in a fit of coughs.

"Jasper, go back." Eden had already left him to help Dane pull the nearest heavy raft toward the water. "Hike to the snowcat and then bring help from McMurdo. Please take Yeti."

"And leave you on your own?" *Not a chance.* "Dane, get out of the way, buddy. Let me at least check this thing for visible cracks."

"That's the spirit." Dane was practically jubilant. If he had to guess, Jasper figured the old dude was far more excited by the prospect of some vast treasure vault than finding his friend.

Jasper took his time inspecting the probably WWII era craft. It seemed solid, but who knew? There could be rapids ahead. One sharp rock could be all it took to kill. During his time as a SEAL, he'd spent plenty of time in cold water, but with proper gear. The three of them didn't have shit. A couple of headlamps that could be picked up for a ten-dollar bill at any sporting goods store and a raft that may or may not keep them dry.

He tossed three life jackets onto the rear bench.

"What's the verdict?" Eden asked.

"Help me get it into the water. Let's at least see if it floats before we get in."

The rubber was a thick as the swastika on the far side was creepy. No matter how compelling the end result might be of possibly reuniting Eden with her dad, this was a seriously bad idea.

"It floats." Dane actually clapped.

Lord . . .

"Looks like we have our answer," Eden redirected her headlamp onto the raft. "Full speed ahead." Before Jasper could stop her, she tossed her pack into the craft, then placed Yeti on the middle seat before climbing in beside him.

"Any sign of it taking on water?" Jasper asked.

"Nope."

He held the craft by an old school jute rope that had seen way better days. "Let me at least change out the guide rope. If we need to tie it off with this crap, it'll never hold." The raft had three wooden seats and a plywood floor—at least it looked like painted plywood. Had they even made it back then? History hadn't been his best subject.

He finished the task sooner than he'd liked. He'd hoped for a miracle to avoid this trip into inky black, but none came.

Dane climbed aboard. "This sure beats walking."

"I'd hold your judgement till we survive the next ten minutes. Dane, do me a favor and keep your light focused on the floor. If you see so much as a drop of water, let me know."

"Sure thing." He used his coat sleeve to brush dust from the seat before sitting.

Jasper shook his head. The guy was a cornball, but he was growing on him.

"Hold on," Jasper coiled the rope in his left hand, then grabbed hold of the raft with his right. He'd performed the maneuver of shoving off with one foot on shore too many times to count, yet this time was the most disconcerting. Never had he had more at stake.

He used an oar to help steer them into the middle of the channel, but the current pretty much took them where it wanted them to go. The humidity made the air dank. Somehow it felt colder than while trudging through wind and snow. This was the kind of cold that sunk deep into his marrow. Never had he wished more to be on his dream beach in the Bahamas.

Yet oddly enough, the deeper they traveled, the warmer it grew.

Parkas were removed and stowed under the bench seats. The raft's floor was thankfully still dry.

"Anyone else hungry?" Jasper asked.

"You're not suggesting we stop for a full meal?" Dane asked.

Eden pulled a protein bar from her pack, passing it back to him. "Will this hold you over until—" She screamed.

He followed her light's direction to see a skeleton propped against a wall. Poor bastard was garbed in full Nazi gear from his crooked hat to dusty black boots.

"How do you think he got here?" Eden asked.

"Maybe he fell off a raft?" Jasper unwrapped the bar, eating half in one bite. "Lost his bearings and with no light, just sat down to die."

She shuddered.

A faint roar made Jasper freeze mid-chew.

Dane looked back. "Is that grumbling rapids up ahead?"

"That would be my guess. Put these on." Jasper tossed Eden and Dane life jackets before strapping one on himself.

A few minutes later, the craft bobbed and shuddered through a downhill chute that left them and their gear soaked.

Yeti howled.

Jasper did his best to avoid a collision, but with boulders the size of Volkswagens, it was inevitable. "Brace yourselves!"

Water cold enough to be liquid ice surged over the low sides, swirling around their feet.

Yeti leapt to Eden's neck.

She cried out from the scratch of his claws. Blood dripped down her back, but she held tight to the little menace.

Dane made the sign of the cross on his chest.

Jasper gritted his teeth. His muscles screamed from the water's force against the ancient wooden paddle. It snapped. And then they were at the water's mercy.

After each surge upward, they crashed down hard. Water cascaded over them, soaking them head-to-toe.

Jasper had been in some bad spots, but this was looking seriously dicey.

Just when he thought their situation couldn't get worse, the water ran even faster. Up ahead, the ceiling height dropped to a mere couple feet of clearance.

"Get down!" he shouted just before the raft's fragile rubber wall ripped against the rock wall.

12

Eden squeezed her eyes shut tight—not that it mattered. She hadn't crouched fast enough to stop her headlamp from smashing against the low rock ceiling. She assumed Dane and Jasper's lights had been hit, too, as their world had gone dark.

Terror welled deep inside her.

The water in the boat now swirled around her knees. It had long since crowned her boots, and the icy liquid numbed her toes.

Was this it? How they would die? All alone in a black tomb.

She'd been consumed by her cancer, but she wouldn't even have that long to live. She regretted not telling Jasper how much she loved him—for she did. All of this was her fault. Everything. Start to finish. If she hadn't called him, he never would have charged to her rescue.

"Everyone all right?" he called, dowsing them in the glow of his back-up penlight.

"I-I think so." She hugged the drenched cat.

"Yes," Dane said. "Are we sinking?"

"It would appear so," Jasper said. "Anyone have anything they could use to bail?" The current had slowed, but they were in a low tube with no way of escaping other than to ride it out—assuming there even was an *out*.

Eden tried keeping panic at bay, but with the water now lapping at her thighs, she didn't have much luck.

"Am I hallucinating?" Dane asked. "Or is that light up ahead?"

"This place just keeps getting weirder . . ." Jasper slowly exhaled. "Everyone hold on for a few more minutes. I think that's a freakin' dock."

The river floated them out of the closed space and into a dimly lit vaulted chamber. Utilitarian wall sconces had been fitted into the rock, and a concrete landing jutted out to greet them.

"How is this possible?" Eden asked, forgetting how cold she was to gape at the domed ceiling. Stalagmites and stalactites and thousands of spindly soda straws vied for top billing in a bragging show of Mother Nature's handiwork when left on her own for thousands of years.

"Geothermal power," Dane said. "It's the only way these lights are possible. I've long heard rumors, but to see that the Germans actually did it? And that the power is still working. I'm in awe. Your father must at least replace bulbs."

"I'm starting to think he really is here." Hope coursed through her, warming limbs that had gone numb.

Jasper tossed a rope lasso around a piling, pulling them in.

Yeti was the first to leap for dry ground.

Dane followed, holding out his hand to help Eden and then Jasper from the raft.

It took all three of them to drag the raft from the water onto the cave floor. The small bit of remaining air seeped out as the hull deflated.

Six rafts stood in a row as they had at the previous stop in this otherworldly labyrinth. Was Dane right? Was this an escape route? Would the river take them further to safety? Or deeper underground?

"Let's set up a camp and dry out." Jasper hefted his pack to higher ground. "We'll eat, rest up, then start fresh in a few hours."

"No," Eden and Dane said in unison.

Eden talked over him, "If my dad is here, I need to find him. He could be hurt."

"Judging by the looks of this place," Jasper said, taking it all in, "he's done far better for himself than we have. Think logically, Eden. We need to at least change into dry clothes before hypothermia sets in."

"Okay," she said, "but then we go."

Arms crossed, he nodded.

She retreated to a dim corner to peel off her unwieldly wet boots, bib overalls and socks to change into dry jeans, socks and sneakers. She felt funny about stripping even to her panties in front of Dane. What had her even more flustered was the sight of Jasper's muscular thighs. A flash of his abs warmed her more effectively than a crackling fire.

"Like what you see?" He winked.

Mouth dry, she hastily looked away.

What was wrong with her? It wasn't as if they hadn't spent entire weekends in bed. They'd explored each other's bodies at leisure. But now, everything had changed. The chemistry between them seemed supercharged and new. What would it be like to be with him again? Would she ever have the chance?

"Ready?" Dane asked. "I'm anxious to get started."

"Let's all have a couple protein bars and some water," Jasper suggested. "I can't imagine what's waiting beyond that door."

They all looked to the rusty steel barrier.

Anticipation bubbled in her chest. As hopeful as she was to find her father, she was also enthralled by their accidental discovery of a secret place time had forgotten.

After eating, they voted to leave their bulky cold-weather gear hanging over an iron rail to hopefully dry. Yes, they were taking a chance in not having it. But wet, the garments would be useless even if needed.

"Who wants to do the honors?" Dane asked with a broad smile, giving the door a Vanna White flourish.

"Go for it," Jasper said.

Dane gave the thick, iron handle a tug. It didn't budge. Reddening, he said, "I suppose I could use a hand."

Jasper stepped in to help. Together, they opened the door with a rusty-hinged creak that echoed through the chamber.

What they found was another tunnel lit by hanging strands of mostly burned out bulbs.

After fifty yards, it branched into another—only with two choices of direction, and even more dead bulbs.

At the next junction, they had three choices. It had grown dark enough for Jasper to turn on his penlight.

"This is a disaster," Dane said. "At this rate, we'll never find the treasure."

"You mean my father?" Eden was more than a little put out that his priorities seemed skewed.

"Yes. Of course." He at least had the good graces to redden.

Yeti stopped in the middle of the trail for a tongue bath.

While Jasper fished through his pack for a tool sharp enough to scrape the rock wall, Eden clasped her locket for the usual comfort it provided, only to get a shock. "Um, guys . . ." Hoping this wasn't a case of her imagination working overtime, she fumbled with the chain's clasp, taking it off to check for herself if what she thought was happening, really was. "Look at this. My locket is suddenly hot—and the amethyst's glowing."

Dane took one look, and clutched the wall for support when his knees buckled. "Do you know why that locket cost your father such an obscene amount of money? It's not merely a locket, but a map. Maybe even a key. See the pattern of the tree's roots? Do they seem familiar?"

"Jasper check it out," she passed it to him. "Dane's right. I never noticed, but the roots are fanning out like a maze of trails. Only one path leads to the stone. We must be close, or it wouldn't be glowing."

"*How* is it glowing?" He turned it over and over again, then opened it for a look inside. "I don't get it. How can something this small have such a complex mechanism inside?"

"I don't know, but it does. We have to follow the map. Help me backtrack so we can figure this out."

It took a while, but they finally learned the pattern to the trails.

Jasper marked each turn, and the closer they were on the map to the stone on the locket, the brighter it glowed.

Their journey had grown so fantastical that no one spoke.

They'd earlier joked about her father being as much of a character as the famed Indiana Jones, but all of this really did feel straight out of a movie—not the sort of thing she'd ever expected to stumble across. As optimistic as she was of whatever fantastic finds were yet to come, she fought a growing anger at her father. How long had he known of this place? Had he taken her mother here before she'd died? If so, why hadn't he told Eden? Had it been a lack of trust? If so, that hurt. Deeper than she ever could have known.

They came to another door. This one, with a locking mechanism that looked far too modern for the rusty Nazi motif.

The key? Judging by the heart-shaped indentation in a panel fixed to the wall, it was obvious.

Hands trembling, palms sweating, pulse out of control, she pressed her locket into the open channel. For five beats of her heart, nothing happened. And then . . .

A mechanism clicked.

An airlock exhaled.

The door creaked open, welcoming them into another world.

13

Jasper had seen a lot of things in his life. He'd dined in a sultan's palace. Shaken the hand of the Commander in Chief. He'd made out with a certain starlet who'd been touring with the USO. But never had he encountered anything quite like this.

The door opened onto a sterile, endless corridor finished in white subway tile that gleamed beneath a row of hanging lights. Classical music floated through the air. Tinny sounding. As if it were far off, yet not quite of this world.

"Stay close." Jasper withdrew the 9mm he'd stashed in the waistband of his jeans. He halfway expected the gnarled form of Hitler himself to step out from one of the closed gray steel doors.

At the end of the hall was another door—this

one a more traditional, dark-stained six-paneled oak. He opened it slowly, pulse pounding, with his gun at the ready, fully prepared to open fire.

If the brightly lit corridor was an odd find this far beneath the earth's surface, what next awaited him was like something out of a dream.

They stepped into a two-story library, complete with a ladder on rails to access thousands of leather-bound books held on intricately carved shelves. The space was as cozy as it was grand—softly glowing Tiffany lamps and a flickering gas-log fireplace with a marble mantel. Thick, exotic-looking rugs absorbed their footfalls and a massive grandfather clock ticked far slower than his heart. The fire meant someone was down here—although not necessarily Eden's father.

How was this real?

How could *any* of this be real?

While Eden turned in a slow circle, drinking it all in, Yeti leapt onto a blue velvet settee.

Dane stood by the nearest bookshelf, carefully turning the pages of a book he'd taken from a stand, staring in awe as if he held a glowing orb. "This is a Gutenberg Bible. Until today, there were forty-eight in the world. Now . . ." He paused for a moment as if to regain his composure before fainting. "There are apparently forty-nine."

Eden strolled through an open door leading to a dining room.

Jasper followed.

The mahogany table would easily seat twenty. The ceiling had been painted sky blue. Cherubs and angels frolicked above. Expensive-looking oil paintings hung in a row. Portraits mixed with old-school food porn.

"These are Rembrandts, Renoirs, Monet's and Manet's . . ." Eden's voice held a reverent tone. "I can't even begin to calculate what these must be worth."

"So the treasure's real?" Jasper asked. "But is this worth killing for?"

He pushed open a swinging door to reveal a kitchen and pantry. Shelves held stacks of china. Tarnished silver goblets and urns and trays. It made him more than a little nauseous to believe full-on Nazi dinner parties must have been held down here.

A wine cellar had been built into the cavern wall—hundreds of dusty bottles visible through a glass door.

"I'm kind of in a stupor." Eden ran her fingers atop a cherry sideboard. "Everywhere I look is something more fabulous. But I should be searching for my dad. He has to be down here, don't you think?"

"Someone sure as hell is." He spied a modern-day mini fridge, plugged with a converter into an ancient wall socket. Inside? Bologna, mayo, dried fruit and a bunch of American cheese and Coke.

Drumming his fingers atop the white marble counter, he grew madder and madder. Like what the hell? How could Eden's dad have known about this and not shared the knowledge with the world? Now, if they weren't careful, that slimeball Leo was going to get his greedy hands on all of it.

"Aren't you a little pissed at your father? Assuming he's the gatekeeper, he has to have been coming down here for years. It's like he's been living a double life. There are probably another couple of entrances, too."

When she remained silent, he figured he'd hit a nerve. Not wishing to rub salt in very fresh wounds, he eased her fingers between his. "Let's finish this, okay? We'll find him, then get the hell out of here."

She swallowed hard. Tears shone in her eyes, but she nodded.

The kitchen was a dead-end, so they walked back through the dining room to the library where Dane was still engrossed in books and Yeti had fallen asleep on a pillow in front of the fire. He purred loud enough for it to be heard across the room.

Jasper held tight to Eden while exploring room after room. Formal living areas and bedrooms fit for royalty. A double-lane bowling alley and a theater. Bathrooms with deep tubs and showers and toilets. Marble sinks with plenty of hot and cold water.

"How is all of this so perfectly preserved?" Eden asked. "How is there no dust?"

"Remember the airlock when we came in? It's sealed. Probably has a special ventilation system with filters in the event of chemical warfare."

They came to a room with a rumpled bed and an open bag of potato chips on the nightstand. Also on the nightstand was a framed photo of Eden when she'd been a little girl. Her mother held her hand.

She gasped, then broke down, collapsing on the side of the bed. "H-How could he? Our friends were murdered in cold blood and f-for what? A dozen paintings and a bunch of musty old books?"

"I'm afraid there's far more to it than that, my beauty."

Jasper whipped around to find Eden's father, Carl, standing in the open doorway. It took every ounce of his restraint not to punch him.

"Dad, h-how could you keep all of this from me?" Despite her anger, she ran to him for a hug. "Did Mom know?"

"Yes." He held tight. "We debated whether or not to tell you, but decided in the end that the burden of carrying this secret was too great. The potential for good is boundless. How else do you think I funded my cancer research? And the station? I'm so close to finding a cure. In the wrong hands, this kind of wealth . . ." He stepped back, ramming his hands in the pockets of wool slacks that looked as if they'd been made in the forties. "The amount of wealth

Hitler and his party accumulated down here isn't just what you must have seen in the formal rooms. That isn't the tip of the iceberg." He held out his hand to her. "Come. I'll show you your legacy."

"There's more?"

"You have no idea . . ."

She took his hand, but then turned to look toward the library. "Wait. We should find Dane. I know he'll want to see."

Her father's gaze narrowed. "You brought Dane?"

She nodded. "He helped save us. Dad, it was horrible. After you left, Leo's men took me hostage. They insisted I knew where to find you and your treasure, but—"

"Well, well, well . . ." Dane entered the room, brandishing the second of the two 9mms Jasper had stowed in his pack. "If it isn't my oldest, dearest friend who's been lying to me for the past two decades. All of those times you were supposedly off studying penguins, you were here, lounging in luxury amongst millions in stolen art, books and antiquities."

"Wait—" Jasper's head was spinning. Dane had been lying to them all along? His initial suspicion not to trust him had been right? Meaning, all this time, in having him near Eden, he'd been putting her directly in harm's way. Meaning, after all these years, his instincts were no better than they'd ever been.

"You're working with Leo?"

Dane smiled. "He and his men should be here any time."

"They can't get in without Eden's locket," Carl said.

Dane waved off Carl's concern. "Of course, they can. I placed a rock on the threshold to keep the door from locking. I was the one who convinced Leo that in this case, a soft sell would be infinitely more successful than manhandling the answer from Eden. And look, I'm happy to say I was right." He stepped behind her, pressing the gun to her head. "Sorry, pet. I really do have a deep affection for you—Jasper, too. But I love money more."

Jasper's stomach roiled. He was close enough to shoot Dane where he stood. But what if in the process, he clipped Eden? No way could he take that chance.

"Jasper," Dane said, "I could have dropped you down that crevasse, but turns out you have brains as well as brawn, which means I'm going to need you to put down your gun and come with me."

"No problem." He set the gun on the bed. *As soon as I get the chance, I'll kill you with my bare hands, you lying sack of shit.*

"Good. I would go ahead and dispose of you now, but that brawn of yours may yet come in handy. Leo and his men are at least an hour behind. They've been tracking me ever since we first met up."

Eden's face turned sickly pale. Her lower lip quivered.

"Dane," Carl said. "It's me you have a problem with. I'm the one who lied. Let Eden and Jasper go."

"Oh right," Dane waved the gun like the madman he'd turned out to be. "And the second they hit McMurdo, they'll send out the cavalry. Not going to happen. Now, where are my manners? Before I so rudely interrupted, you were about to show your daughter her legacy. Since I'm part of the family, I would like to see it, too."

"Very well." Resigned to the fact that Dane wouldn't easily go away, Carl gestured for them to follow him out of his bedroom and down another corridor. They exited the formal area through a second airlock. This time, they didn't emerge into another part of the cavern, but at the top of an enormous flight of stairs. A metal rail had been attached to the sweating cave wall.

"Well?" They'd all bunched on the landing, but using his gun, Dane waved them along. "What are we waiting for? I'm ready to see my treasure."

Jasper counted fifteen flights before they reached the lower landing. A vault door—the type he'd only seen in old bank robber movies—was closed. It had a combination lock and wheeled handle.

"What's the combo?" Dane asked.

"You'll have to shoot me before I tell you."

"Fine." Without hesitation, Dane shot Carl's foot.

Eden screamed.

Blood splattered everywhere. On the floor and vault door. Most alarmingly, all over Eden's clothes and face.

She went to her father, dropping to her knees to inspect his badly bleeding foot. "You're horrible!" she screamed at Dane. "I loved you. How could you be so cruel?"

Jasper dragged his sweatshirt over his head to use as a bandage that would hopefully, at least slow Carl's bleeding.

"You think me cruel? Your father not only hoarded whatever's behind this door for himself, just as he took your mother. Did he ever tell you that she wanted me first? He stole her from me—just as he did all of my professional glory. I'm done being his second. Now, it's my turn to be on top."

"You forgot one thing!" At the top of the stairs, Leo, flanked by his men, stood on the upper landing. "You're paid by me! Kill him. He's outlasted his usefulness."

The man nearest him raised his M16 and shot a single bullet into Dane's chest. Blood gurgled from his mouth.

Eden cried out, sharply looking away.

Dane collapsed, falling into a pool of his own blood.

"Quickly," Carl said. "Get me to the vault."

Eden and Jasper helped him reach the lock. He worked the combination while Leo and his men charged down the stairs. Their hard-soled footsteps echoed through the vast space. "Jasper, please pull."

The door weighed as much as a small car Jasper had once helped eight other guys move as a prank. Once it swung open wide enough for Carl to hobble through, Eden and Jasper followed, giving the door a mighty tug to close it behind them. Only then did Jasper fear what he'd done.

They were now locked into a chamber that could for all he knew be airtight.

The darkness was as complete as the silence.

Jasper took his penlight from his back pocket, shining it at Eden and Carl's pale faces. "Everyone okay?"

Eden nodded.

"I'll manage," Carl said. "Jasper, to the right of the vault door is the overhead light switch. Would you please be so kind as to turn it on?"

He did. And then damn near fainted himself.

What he faced wasn't a mere treasure, but an obscene hoard. The result of looting entire countries of their heritage and wealth. The cathedral of riches stretched as long as a football field and half as wide. There were piles upon piles of gold bullion. Egyptian statues and bejeweled sarcophaguses. Roman and Greek sculptures. Cases filled with jewels and crowns and scepters. Still more cases held gold and silver coins. A hundred open crates held gold-framed paintings.

Eden's mouth hadn't closed since Jasper had flipped on the lights.

"I told you," Carl said. "All of this is for you. Together, we'll find a cure for the cancer that killed your mother. We'll vindicate her, then save millions of others."

"It's too late," she whispered.

"No . . ." His bright-eyed hope faded. "I couldn't save your mother, but I will save you."

"I couldn't agree more," Jasper said, "but first, please tell me there's another way out of here? Leo and his guys aren't screwing around. I already used a couple of their rocket launchers that I'm sure would work fine for blowing your vault door to kingdom come."

His eyes widened. "What did you use them for?"

"Dad, it doesn't matter. Is there a way out? Dane said Hitler always had an escape route."

"He did. But what about the treasure? We can't leave it. We'll need to keep selling it off bit-by-bit to fund the cure. *Your* cure."

She shook her head. "Please, let's just go. I'm cold and hungry and want to go home."

"Yes. *Home.*" As if resigned to his defeat, Carl reached for an emerald-topped cane to help him reach the vault's rear entry. He'd just reached the lock when an explosion knocked him to his knees.

14

Eden's ears bled from the force of the blow. The ringing was so loud she struggled to form coherent thoughts.

Where were Jasper and her father?

"Carl?" Leo shouted. "Come out, come out, wherever you are! You've hidden from me long enough, old friend. Time to die!"

Eden spotted her father on the concrete floor, lying next to Jasper.

Her heart caught in her throat. Were they both dead?

Careful to stay out of Leo's line of sight, she crawled to Jasper, covering his heart with her hand. It blessedly beat strong beneath her palm. "Jasper?" She gave him a gentle nudge. "Talk to me. I need you. *Please*, wake up."

He eked his eyes open. "What happened?"

"Leo bulldogged his way into the vault. We have about two minutes before he finds us. Think you can not only move, but help me with my father?"

He nodded.

"Dad," she crouched beside him, "you have to wake up. We need the combo to the back door.

"E-Eva Braun's birthday . . ."

"I don't know when that is." She looked to Jasper. "Do you?"

"What do you think?"

She looked to her father, but he'd passed out cold.

Leo shouted, "Come out, come out wherever you are!" He punctuated his sentence by firing off a few rounds.

"This is a serious longshot," she said, "but I swear once my mom told me I shared the same birthday with Babe Ruth, Bob Marley, and Ronald Reagan. She said there was a famous woman, too, but that since she'd not been treated so nice by history we wouldn't mention her. What if my birthday is hers?"

"February 6?"

She nodded. "But the vault combination takes six digits. So we have 2-6-1-9—and then nothing."

"How old was she when she died? We'll count backwards."

Leo shot again. From much closer. "Come out, kiddies. Time to play!"

Jasper was already at the combination lock, trying different numbers.

She tried focusing on the numbers, but she couldn't hear her own thoughts over the racket of Leo and his men essentially partying with the treasure. Even from fifty yards away, their laughter and shouts echoed throughout the enormous vault. Through the crack between the two cases of art she hid behind, Eden watched two men play catch with gold bars. Another pair threw gold coins at each other. One guy had draped himself in jewels.

Leo, however, looked to be searching for them. He shot again. The bullet dislodged a rock in the cavern ceiling, causing a small avalanche of stone.

"Dad, you have to talk louder," she begged with a growing sense of urgency.

"Got any more ideas?" Jasper asked. "None of these are working."

Her father drifted in and out of consciousness.

"Think, babe. Maybe your dad once gave you a clue, and you didn't even know. Is there anything else special about the locket?"

Leo shot the ceiling again. This time, rocks fell closer.

It was impossible to think with her heart beating so hard it hurt deep within her ribs.

Not bothering with the clasp, she jerked the

locket from her neck, studying the intricate pattern. The tree had twelve branches at the top. Twelve roots at the bottom. "Try 1924!"

"No!"

More gunfire. Significantly more falling rocks on their end of the cavern.

She breathed so erratically that the lack of oxygen affected her vision. "Twelve! Try twelve!"

Rapid-fire machine gun bullets shredded the rock directly above her head. Did Leo know exactly where they were and was just screwing with them?

"*Holy shit!* It worked. Come on!"

"I can't. Not without my father."

In a heartbeat, Jasper was back beside her. Together they dragged her dad from the cavern and into another rock tunnel similar to the one they'd encountered many times before in this strange place.

Jasper slammed the vault door closed behind them, twisting the handle and lock mechanism. Hopefully, buying them time.

"L-leave me," her dad said.

"Not a chance." Jasper slung him over his shoulder just as another explosion shook the ground at their feet. Rocks rained from the ceiling. "*Run!*"

The tunnel led up and up, spiraling in a dizzying pattern.

She made the mistake of glancing back to find the tunnel collapsing behind them. Not only was the sight terrifying, but her soul wept for the lost history. Would any of the mythical bunker and treasure vault survive?

"Yeti!" she cried past searing lungs. "We forgot him."

"Babe . . ." Running uphill while carrying her father had taken a toll on Jasper. His breathing sounded raspy. "Let's save us first—then, the cat. For all we know, that whole section of the compound is gone."

She nodded, but once again, tears stung her eyes. Yeti was just a cat—a cat she hadn't even known all that long. But when she'd already lost so much, his furry life mattered.

On and on they trudged until reaching a steel door.

Eden tugged it open. The sudden change in pressure popped her ears. Ignoring the pain, she trudged through.

Just like that, they were back in the first corridor—the one with the subway tiles and all the doors.

"Let's get you and your dad in a raft, then I'll double back for the cat."

She charged ahead to open the next door that led to the dock where they'd landed. It seemed like days earlier, but could only have been a couple hours. Every muscle in her body screamed, but she kept moving, yanking with all her might on the rope holding the row of rafts in place.

After setting her father on the dirt floor, Jasper

handed her a knife. "Pick a lucky raft, then slash the rest. If Leo and his guys survived that explosion, I don't want them following."

She did as he'd asked.

Ten endless minutes later, two gunshots echoed through the cavern.

She froze. Was Jasper hurt?

Not thinking, just following her every screaming instinct, she jerked open the rusty-hinged door, then charged down the hall as fast as her lungs allowed. "Jasper?"

He emerged from the library at a dead run. "Go! Hurry! Leo's guards are everywhere. Like cockroaches." He held the cat beneath one arm and a sealed wooden case under the other.

She'd already dragged the boat to the water and transferred the good rope from their first ride to the new one.

"You're awesome." He kissed her while passing off Yeti who was still warm. Had he never moved from his spot by the fire? Jasper also handed her his package. "Can you believe the little monster slept through everything?"

"What's this?" she asked.

"The Bible. I figured we could use all the Heavenly help we can get."

She stood on her tiptoes to kiss him again. As always when their lips touched, a rush of pleasure surged through her—head to toes.

He hefted her father into the raft, then held it at the lapping water before hurrying her aboard. He snatched two paddles and three life jackets from a hook on the wall, as well as all of their winter gear and a box similar to the one they'd last seen marked with a red cross.

"Ready?" he asked.

She nodded.

Unconscious again, her father lay on the raft's floor, leaning against her knees.

"No guarantees where this might take us—if anywhere at all."

"I understand." Tears stung her eyes. The river could lead to safety or certain death. Why was it that lately, all roads led to bad places? Was this fate's way of preparing her for the inevitable end soon to come?

The door burst open.

Nausea gripped Eden's stomach.

"Not so fast," Leo said with three thugs behind him. "How can you even think of leaving without saying a proper goodbye?"

Jasper shoved off the raft and leapt in.

"Kill them!" Leo commanded.

Shots echoed through the chamber, ricocheting off the rock walls. The noise was deafening. Then came the rumble of not just another landslide, but what Eden feared might be the last of them all.

As the boat's rubber sides deflated, the river's

current ferried them into darkness. Into certain death.

Dangerously cold water sloshed around their ankles, slithering insidiously higher.

"I love you," she said through teeth chattering from the icy water's all-too-familiar bite.

"Love you, babe. Don't give up."

"I-I won't." She clung to Yeti, selfishly wishing he were Jasper.

A terrifying roar grew closer and closer until their craft bobbed in black terror. With no light, all she had was the sound of what little remained of their ride being hurled against boulders.

"Give me your hand!" Jasper called above the water's crashing.

In the absolute darkness, she fumbled behind her for that primal connection.

They might have five minutes to live or five seconds. All she knew was that she was selfishly beyond grateful to spend that time with him.

The current pushed faster and faster.

The water in their sinking boat rose higher and higher.

All she could do in the face of certain death was to squeeze Jasper's hand, praying the end came blessedly swift.

15

"Jasper! Come on, buddy. Talk to me."

Jasper winced from the glare of sun. "Eden?" He sat up, only to grab his aching forehead and drop back down. For the first time in forever, he wasn't cold. And far from being trapped in a dark cave, sunlight streamed across the foot of a proper bed. "Wait—Harding? What the hell are you doing in Antarctica?"

"What do you think? Saving your miserable ass. Nash, Everett, Briggs, Raleigh, Jackson and Sawyer—we're all here. Well, I'm *here*. Everyone else is in the chow hall. You know we've always got your back."

Jasper snorted. "You're a little late. Where the hell am I? And where's Eden? And her dad? Oh—

and her cat."

"They're all fine. In rooms next to yours. We're at McMurdo. When we didn't hear from you, we got worried. I set wheels in motion and stumbled into one helluva mess. You sure know how to pick 'em. Here, I thought you were ditching work for a romantic rendezvous, and lo and behold you pop the cherry on a conspiracy that's got the whole world riveted."

"Wait—how did you even find us? How long have I been out?"

"Dude—you had an entire fringe army of Neo-Nazi's on your tail. Once we found them, it was easy enough to find you. There aren't a lot of places to hide down here. Plus, these douchebags have been leaving a trail of death. We've found a couple entrances to the underground compound—what was left of you and your raft washed up on the shore of the Ross Sea. We're still trying to figure out where you popped out at. The compound itself is pretty eff'd up from itchy trigger fingers and too many plastic explosives. A worldwide team of eggheads are itching to get in there when engineers give it an all clear on safety. You're lucky you made it out with only hypothermia and a frost-bitten little toe."

"Did they amputate?"

Harding grinned. "Nah. Relax. You're still pretty as ever for your girl."

"Speaking of which . . ." Jasper sat up again, and

this time stayed up long enough to get out of the bed and onto his feet. Someone had dressed him in sweats and thick white socks. "I need to see Eden."

"Sure. She's right next door."

Jasper wandered that direction. He was achy as hell, but otherwise okay.

He entered Eden's room and found her sleeping.

When he swept her hair back from her eyes, she woke with a start.

"Sorry, babe. Didn't mean to scare you."

Like he'd been, she seemed dazed and disoriented. "Where are we? Are you okay? Where are my dad and Yeti?"

"Good. Everyone's real good." He relayed the same information Harding had given him.

"I thought we were dead."

"I know, right?" He pulled over a chair to sit next to her bed. "But we're not. So look . . ." He forced a deep breath. "I know this may not be the time or place, but what we just went through taught me to stop waiting for the *right* time to tell you some things, because it may never come. We got lucky, babe. That has to mean something. I want you to go back to your doctor—or hell, find a new doctor. *Please*, fight this disease the way you have fought Leo and his guys. I know what you went through with your mom was rough, but medicine's come a long way since then. Together, we can beat this. I know we can. At the very least, we should try. I love you.

I've got issues to work on back home, but after that, let's get married."

She said nothing. She didn't make eye contact with him or even breathe. What did that mean?

"Talk to me. What are you thinking?"

"You should probably go."

"Wait—what?"

"I-I have a ton of stuff to think about. I need space. The last thing you need is to be saddled with a sick woman who has no hope of—"

"That's BS and you know it. After what we just survived, how can you say there's no hope?"

"Jasper, *please*, just go. I can't be with you. That's final."

Jaw clenched hard enough to hurt, Jasper realized he'd run out of things to say. The woman was as tough as she was stubborn. She knew he loved her. She knew he'd do anything to save her from any outside force.

The one thing he couldn't save her from was herself.

Two days later, McMurdo's doc deemed Jasper healthy enough to travel, so Jasper and his team hopped the next available flight.

He sat sandwiched between Briggs and Everett

on the routine five-and-a-half hour C-130 trip to Christchurch, New Zealand.

Briggs noshed pretzels and listened to metal the whole way and Everett listened to cry-in-your-beer country while playing Mahjong on his phone.

Which left Jasper with too much time to think.

He felt stuck in a *Twilight Zone* episode from which he couldn't escape.

He left his seat to hit the john, and then he saw her—seated at the opposite end of the massive ride.

Her dad sat beside her with his bad foot elevated.

A woman he recognized as a nurse from the medical center took his vitals.

Yeti slept in a makeshift carrier tucked beneath Eden's seat.

Strange how in the center of the violent storm they'd been caught up in, these people had been his family. Now they were strangers. What happened? He thought she loved him. Had he never really known her at all?

They landed.

Collected gear.

Harding had arranged for transportation to a B & B he'd rented for the whole crew until their next day's flight. The place was all decked out for Christmas. He'd forgotten the holiday was even near.

While the guys settled in for beer and poker, Jasper begged off. He stripped, grabbed a quick hot shower, then pulled down blackout shades before climbing into bed.

He'd had enough eternal sun.

He was just drifting off when the door opened, and then closed. "Briggs? That you?"

He couldn't see anything, but heard rustling.

"Everett? If you're trying to convince me this place is haunted, it isn't working."

A warm, silky all-woman's body slid beside him under the covers. When she cozied closer, one inhalation of her familiar breath told him Eden had finally come to her senses.

"Babe . . ."

"Shh. I don't want to talk. I just want to feel."

He had no problem with that—especially, when she eased lower, taking him into her mouth.

Eyes closed, he combed his fingers through her long loose hair, groaning as she worked him just the way he liked. They had history. Great history. It was about time she understood where he was coming from.

They belonged together.

End of story.

Just before he'd reached his breaking point, she rolled on a condom she must have brought, then straddled him. He thrust upward while clasping his hands to her hips, pushing her down. He couldn't get deep enough. He wanted to swallow her whole.

She leaned forward, brushing her hard nips

against his chest. Raw sensation roared through him like a freaking jackhammer. With his hand at the back of her head, he kissed her rougher than he probably should have, then rolled her over to slam back into her even harder. She bucked her hips, meeting him thrust for thrust. Moaning with each push.

He was kissing her, kissing her. Drinking her soul.

He reached down to finger her and knew by the way she shuddered that she'd come. He worked harder to make her rise and fall again.

When he couldn't hold back a second longer, he arched and then froze while the world stood still for one solitary moment of sheer perfection.

And then the act was done.

And awkwardness barged between them as effectively as if it were another person in the room.

Crying, she slipped out from under the covers, dashed to the bathroom and slammed the door.

Shit.

He left the bed, wadded the condom in a tissue. Banged on the bathroom door. "You're not playing fair."

"Sorry. I wanted to feel you inside me, one last time."

He rested his forehead against the cool wood door. "Did it ever occur to you that we could get married and then spend a lifetime humping like bunnies?"

The door opened. "I'm scared."

He pulled her into his arms, wrapping her tight enough for her to hopefully realize this was where she belonged. "I'm scared. I could get shot on my next assignment. Or hit by a car. Just because your mother died of cancer, that doesn't mean you will, too. Think about what we've been through. Do you honestly think having chemo treatments could be tougher than escaping a madman while trapped on a sinking raft in a dark, ice cube of a river?"

"When you put it that way . . ."

"Exactly." He took her hands, easing his fingers between hers. "So we're going to do this? Kick cancer's ass?"

While she nodded against his chest, Jasper prayed his tough talk would be enough to see her safely through this war for which he had no weapon other than love.

16

Eden had never been to Montana, but the closer Jasper drove them toward his family home, the more excited—and nervous—she grew.

He didn't look much better. He was easily the most gorgeous man she'd ever seen, but the grim set of the lips she loved kissing told a sad story while he handled the wheel of his black Jeep Wrangler.

A light snow fell. Not enough to cover the highway. Just enough to remind her of their time in Antarctica, and of how glad she was to be back in a place where spring and summer were right around the calendar's corner.

Her father had wanted to tag along to meet Jasper's family, but he was still recovering while writing a book about his Nazi discovery.

He was staying in the guest house of the ancient Victorian home she and Jasper were restoring back in Denver.

Three months had passed since her surgery and treatments and so far, so good. She'd had twinges of nausea, but medication and plenty of saltines and Sprite and love had gotten her through. At her last check-up, she was officially announced cancer free, and she and Jasper would be married in Aspen in June.

She'd faced her cancer issue head-on, but she feared Jasper's trouble with his parents and older brother only loomed larger. Which was why she'd made him promise to invite his folks and brother to the wedding. When he refused, she'd coaxed his buddy Briggs into finding Jasper's mother's number. The initial conversation had been beyond awkward, but it had been a start.

Maybe this would be the weekend that once again made Jasper whole.

"Tell me about Mariah," she asked.

"Don't. You know this is the last place I want to be. Talking about old wounds won't make them better. What I did was beyond shitty. I don't deserve to ever have them talk to me again."

"It wasn't so long ago when you were telling me to face my darkest fear. Why can't you do the same? It's been a long time. What if all those years have healed old wounds? Your mom, at least, seemed relieved to hear you're alive."

He took her hand, kissing each finger. "How could she ever forgive me? I was an idiot kid— seventeen. I not only thought it was a great idea to dare my sister-in-law into using Ecstasy to celebrate her anniversary, but it turned out to be a bad batch and she died. I trusted my friend to get me good stuff—" he snorted "—how much is wrong with that statement? Then look what happened with Dane. I trusted him and he damn near got us both killed."

"Stop." She rubbed his tight neck. "What happened with your sister-in-law was another lifetime. You're a changed man. Plus, no one forced her to take the drug. As for Dane, he fooled me, too. I'm hurt, but getting over it. All we can do is surround ourselves with good people and hope for the best." Leaning over to kiss his cheek, she added, "As soon as we get the all-clear from my doctor, I can't wait to make an awesome father out of you."

"From your lips to God's ears, babe." They finished the last thirty miles in silence.

When Jasper left the main road to turn on to a dirt, pine tree-lined drive, she took deep breaths to calm her nerves.

Her fiancé gripped the wheel so hard his knuckles shone white.

"It's going to be okay," she said. "You'll see."

He nodded, but didn't look convinced.

The house was a two-story rustic, log cabin. This time of year, the boxes under each window were barren, but Eden imagined them filled with geraniums. A wide front porch held six rockers. A pinecone wreath on the front door said *Welcome* in pretty scrolled letters.

Jasper parked the Jeep, but didn't turn off the engine. "I can't do this."

"Excuse me . . ." She cleared her throat. "What did you say to me when I was afraid to have surgery and my chemo?"

"That's different."

"How? Clearing cancer from our lives is no more important than you clearing this past shame from yours? What are you going to tell our future son or daughter when they ask to spend a weekend at their grandma and grandpa's house?"

A muscle ticked in his clean-shaven jaw.

"Come on, sweetie. You can do this."

A woman stepped out of the front door. She was plump, with salt and pepper hair. She wore a pretty floral blouse and jeans, covered by a frilly apron. After taking one look in the car, she burst into tears, then came at them at a full run.

Jasper left the Jeep and squeezed his mom in an epic hug.

A graying man Eden assumed was his dad left the porch to join them, as did an older, weathered version of Jasper who could only be his big brother.

Eden swallowed back her own tears, blinking her stinging eyes as she left the vehicle to take in the touching family reunion.

"I'm so sorry," Jasper said with heartbreaking sobs. "So, so sorry. I never meant to—"

"We know," his father said.

A very pregnant woman emerged from the house. She brought a box of tissues outside and passed it around. "I'm Leah, Kyle's wife. Mind if I get in on this action?"

"Wait—you remarried?" Jasper looked to his brother.

"If you'd bothered to give us your contact information, we would have invited you to the ceremony. Life's too short for grudges, baby brother. Losing Mariah taught me every second counts." Kyle looked to Eden. "You ever planning on introducing us to the pretty lady wearing your ring?"

Jasper conked his forehead, then left his family to slip his arm around her waist, guiding her over. "This is Eden. We're going to be married in June. It would mean the world to us if you'd all come."

They agreed, and Eden walked arm-in-arm into the home where the love of her life had grown up. In the big country kitchen, a plate of homemade sugar cookies sat on the counter and the air smelled of pot roast and all the trimmings—heavenly.

While Jasper jogged out to the car for Yeti, Eden accepted the seat Jasper's dad had offered at the kitchen table. She had the oddest sensation that her mother was with her now, smiling down on her, happy that her daughter had not only found the perfect man, but a perfect forever home.

EPILOGUE

Ψ

"Don't peek. This needs to be done right or we'll have seven years of bad luck." Jasper carried Eden from their rental car to the house's porch and was beyond excited about finally showing off the slice of paradise he'd bought them. Sure, he'd had to use the internet and it had been an impulse buy, but how long had he been dreaming of owning his own beach home in the Bahamas?

Their wedding had been beyond perfection with his brother serving as the best man. His mother and Leah had helped Eden get ready and by the time she reached the aisle, she'd been the most spellbinding bride in the history of brides. All of his SEAL buddies had been in attendance, and Eden hit it off great with Nash's wife Maisey and their baby boy.

"I'm pretty sure that seven year rule only applies to breaking mirrors—not honeymoon protocol."

"Whatever." He had a tough time wrangling the key into the lock, but once he did, he opened the door to Paradise. Just as he'd requested, the Realtor had gotten the place ready. There were bowls of fruits and vases overflowing with tropical flowers. Just beyond open glass doors was their very own private beach, complete with a few coconut palms. "Okay, open your eyes."

She said nothing.

He set her to her feet. "What's the matter? I thought you'd love it?"

"I do love it. It's incredible. But I can't even imagine how much this costs to rent. We have medical bills and the house needs a new furnace and you know we should be saving up to add a nursery, and—"

He kissed her quiet. "Relax. Just think of this as a gift from some ancient kings to you."

"You didn't?"

"Grab a few pieces of all that treasure?" He grinned. "Not that it wasn't tempting, but no. Your father, on the other hand, slipped me a princely sum for our engagement present. He said it was your dowry, but that I was only allowed to spend it on something fun."

"So instead of asking me what I wanted, you took it upon yourself to buy us our own isolated beachfront house in the Bahamas?"

"Um, yeah. That's sort of how it went down. You mad?"

She tossed her arms around his neck, kissing him until they had to pause for air. "Madly in love." Stepping back, she tugged her sundress over her head and kicked off her sandals. "Last one in the water's a rotten egg!"

"No fair. You started stripping before I even knew there was a challenge!"

She blew him a kiss before sprinting off to the bathtub-warm aqua water.

He'd just pulled his T-shirt over his head when his cell rang. "No way."

He wanted to ignore it, but the alert tone only sounded when Harding called from the company line. His boss wouldn't be bugging him unless it was an emergency. Considering the fact that his SEAL brothers had not so long ago saved his and Eden's life, Jasper felt honor-bound to answer the call.

"Yo. What's up?"

"Bro, I hate doing this to you," Harding said, "but shit's going down."

"Things were fine when everyone left the wedding."

"Yeah, well, when Nash and Maisey got home, they had an uninvited guest waiting. This guy jumped Maisey and took the baby. She's still unconscious. Nash is with her at the hospital. We need to get a team together *now* to get back their baby boy."

"Is this a ransom thing?"

"Worse. Remember the drug lord we took out? Vicente Rodriguez?"

"Kinda hard to forget. I saw him with my own eyes. Dude was an ugly corpse."

"True," Harding said. "But turns out his wife back in Colombia not only wants to raise her husband's son, but she's out for blood. Her errand boy left a note in the baby's crib that basically said she won't rest until the man and woman she blames for killing the love of her life and stealing her son are dead."

Ready for more SEAL Team: Disavowed? Everett and Ruby's story, SHUNNED, is available now. Please keep reading for an exclusive sneak peek . . .

SHUNNED

SEAL Team: Disavowed Book 3

1

Piapoco, Colombia

The baby was a fake.

Disavowed Navy SEAL Everett Black snatched the doll out of the crib by its shaggy black hair, pitching it across the dark room where it fell with a soft thump against thick carpet. What was he going to tell Nash and Maisey? They'd trusted him to come to Colombia, break into Vicente Rodriguez's widow's heavily guarded compound and take back their kidnapped son.

What now?

Pulse revved, he darted his gaze about the typical nursery. Crib. Changing table. Rocking chair. What was he missing? Was this whole scene a set-up? Had the infant ever been in the freaking castle this chick called home? Or was the intel Trident, Inc. had been given misinformation? Meaning the Widow Rodriguez had been one step ahead of them since the baby had been snatched twenty-four hours earlier.

Gauzy curtains floated in the light breeze.

Time for him to fly.

He'd report his findings to Harding and the rest of the team, then lay low until receiving further instructions.

After sticking the decoy baby back in the crib to hopefully hide the fact that he'd ever been there, Everett pushed aside the curtains to straddle the windowsill.

Since free climbing was kinda his thing, it was no biggie to maneuver himself sideways onto the third floor ledge, then use the limestone mansion's elaborate sills and moldings for handholds. He'd earlier run a dummy signal through the security system, making it feel nice and cozy the whole time he'd been breaking and entering. He'd remotely switch it back once he got clear.

Everett reached the second-floor ballroom's

balcony when a metallic click caught his attention. He froze.

He hadn't worn NVGs, partly because the moon was nearly full and he didn't figure he'd need them. Mostly, because he'd been afraid Baby Joe would have taken one look at "Uncle Everett" in scary monster glasses and freaked. Now, he wished he had them so he could make out the noise's source.

Only when he heard muffled voices did he start to sweat.

June in Colombia was no joke, but up until now, adrenaline had kept him cool. There hadn't been time to do a thorough study of guard activity, but intel said there were three rotating crews of eight-man security teams twenty-four seven. Two guards monitored the house, and six watched the grounds. Thus far, they'd done a piss-poor job, considering he had yet to see one.

Odds were in his favor that the noise he'd heard had been one of the regular patrols making rounds.

When he didn't hear another sound save for a gazillion bugs' rhythmic hums, he figured he was free to scale the last floor, then hightail it through the jungle to the Jeep he'd earlier stashed three miles from the compound.

Antsy to make a quick entrance, Everett braced his palms on the balcony's stone rail, then vaulted himself over.

At that instant, a blinding beam spotlighted him.

"¡Al ladrón!"

Translation? *Shit.*

He grabbed for the next handhold just as shots were fired. One pinged close enough for him to see sparks.

Blinded, pulse racing, he sucked in a deep breath and hoped for the best as he reached blindly for his next perch. What he got was a freefall, a seriously not good twist to his left knee, then, when he tried standing on it, he fell ass-backwards onto the manicured lawn.

He tried hopping up, but screaming pain sent him crashing down again.

Adding to the party were a circle of at least a dozen seriously armed commando-types holding M16s and headlamps aimed at him.

He groaned. Why had he made this a solo mission?

"What a wonderful surprise," a smoky female voice said in a thick Spanish accent.

The lights in his eyes made it too bright to see Jack.

"I do love a party. Although next time, please call first." He couldn't see her, but her perfume was cloying—choking him with the crisp floral scent of high maintenance. "Take him away. See that he has medical attention for his knee. He'll make a nice trade for that bitch who killed my husband."

Ready for more? Everett and Ruby's story,
SHUNNED, is available now.

Dear Reader—

I can't thank you enough for spending time with Jasper and Eden. Hope you loved their story!!

As a huge fan of action-adventure novels by authors like James Rollins and Clive Cussler, I've always dreamed of creating my own high-stakes treasure hunt. In OUTCAST, my wish finally came true! But you know that old saying about being careful what you wish for? LOL!! For a while, it seemed like every line needed to be researched. Not only did I need to learn about Antarctica's weather, wildlife, and landscape, but the scientists who make this wild and hauntingly isolated part of the world their home. To understand more about this little-known place, I highly recommend the documentary, *Antarctica: A Year on Ice*. I was especially intrigued by the hearty souls who "winter over", going months without seeing sun. I would dearly love to experience this, so if anyone has connections, please let me know!!

My favorite bit of research came about while studying Nazi conspiracy theories. It's fact that after WWII, vast caches of stolen art and treasures were located and returned to its rightful owners. But to this day, many priceless artifacts and millions—maybe even, billions—of dollars in gold and treasure are still out there, waiting to be found . . .

The next book in my SEAL Team: Disavowed

series is called, SHUNNED. It opens with the heartbreaking realization that Nash and Maisey from ROGUE, have had their baby kidnapped by drug lord Vicente Rodriguez's widow who is hellbent on avenging her husband's death. With Maisey in a coma and Nash constantly by her side, it's up to team member and friend Everett Black to rescue Baby Joe. What Everett never expects to find during this dangerous quest is forbidden love with Ruby Morales—a novice nun.

Happy Reading—Laura Marie

P.S. If you enjoyed OUTCAST, pretty please leave a review on the site where you purchased it or Goodreads. (Both if you'd really love to make me smile!!)

ABOUT THE AUTHOR

Laura Marie Altom is the author of over fifty novels. Her award-winning work has appeared on numerous bestseller lists and worldwide, she has nearly two million books in print. Laura lives in Tulsa, Oklahoma with her husband of twenty-seven years. This former teacher has been blessed with boy/girl twins and a menagerie of dogs and cats. For fun, Laura's content to garden, thrift-shop or curl up with a great book.

Laura loves hearing from readers, and can be reached at the following social media outlets:

E-mail balipalm@aol.com
Website: www.lauramariealtom.com
Facebook: www.facebook.com/LauraMarieAltom
Twitter: @LauraMarieAltom
Instagram: www.instagram.com/lauramariealtom
Pinterest: www.pinterest.com/lauramariealtom

www.ingramcontent.com/pod-product-compliance
Lightning Source LLC
Chambersburg PA
CBHW021040130626
46552CB00005B/1940